I0545405

A Name Writ In Water

A Name Writ In Water

Keats' last journey

Richard Boden

red hand
BOOKS

First published in 2019 by

Red Hand Books
Kemp House, 152 - 160 City Road,
London
EC1V 2NX

www.redhandbooks.co.uk

All rights in the works printed here revert to the author
and original copyright holders after publication

Copyright©2019 by Richard Boden

ISBN   978 191 0346 389

All rights reserved. No part of this edition may be used
or reproduced in any manner whatsoever without the
prior written permission of the copyright holder,
except in the case of brief quotations embedded
in critical articles or reviews.

A CIP catalogue record for this book is
available from the British Library

Prepared for publication by Red Hand Books
Cover design © Red Hand Books

This book is sold subject to the condition that it shall not
by way of trade or otherwise be lent, re-sold, hired out, or
otherwise circulated without the publisher's prior consent
in any form of binding or cover other than that which it is
published and without a similar condition including this
condition being imposed on the subsequent purchaser.

To

Sarah

PART ONE

The Bay

Naples, October 1820

At first, there was nothing much to make out. The four of them kept squinting, to little purpose, at a po-faced, billowing murk, which kept on staring back. Pressed into hoping, they'd dragged themselves up from their ragged sleep to take in what was supposed to have taken them aback. Or so the captain had said. But yet again, no such luck. Perhaps it would soon burn off.

The only surprise, apart from the cold, was that they'd cared enough to come up on deck and see for themselves. It was, after all, the end of October; the end of a whole month of sleeplessness and seasickness, tense with disappointments. No wonder, when they realized there was nothing more than mist to be seen, that they'd shuffled stiffly back to the line of chairs arranged for them as usual, as if in some private box outdoors.

1

Without saying anything worthwhile, the four of them paired off as usual, the two men and the two women, always separate, as though still wary of each other. After everything they'd been through.

They exchanged their polite good mornings before settling back to silence. The vapours swirled around them. The same, tired things sprang to mind. Severn couldn't settle, far too eager and unsteady, impatient for something to happen. He kept on dabbing at the corners of his mouth with the back of his hairless hand. Next to him, Keats stared dully ahead. None of this bore thinking about. After a while, trying to get comfortable in his oversized woollen coat, he stretched out his legs and, half-forgetting the company he was in, stifled an exuberant yawn.

Miss Cotterell couldn't help but follow suit, smiling at the involuntary nature of things. Looking down, she inspected her hands, rubbed at the rough skin flaking off her knuckles. Under her sensible coat, though no one else knew it, she wore a nice, newish dress, the plum-coloured one with the high, white collar that she'd kept back especially. She, more than any of them, felt the brush of cold on her lips, knew the risk she was taking by being out there. The shivering could start up at any time. More than any of them, she was inclined to make a little talk, but the gentlemen showing no sign of wanting to take her up, she folded her hands in her lap and peered dutifully out, saving her strength. To her

2

left, Mrs Pidgeon, the chaperone, was evidently saying nothing, her eyes squarely fixed on the yardarm and no further. Then, just when Miss Cotterell had had enough and was on the point of retiring, that familiar, faint disturbance, that troubling and lightening which sent a whisper through the mist, that first rumour of sunrise: wonder really was coming.

Severn was first to the rail; Miss Cotterell needed helping up. In a line, they pressed together, elbows touching, Keats' hand on Severn's shoulder. The captain and the watch blurred to murmurs. Below them, the inky sea tingled. The little mist remaining bloomed, lingered plaintively, then disappeared for good. Looking up, Severn could just make out, far off, the last of the hesitant stars, backing and bowing out, like obsequious courtiers, eager to be seen to be discreet, awaiting the king's forthcoming triumph. In fact, the whole sky now seemed naturally tensed, as if preparing itself for all the blue it could hold, all its infinite gradations. The sails, too, getting wind of what they might achieve, blushed and began to puff themselves up, stirring just enough to be accused of putting on airs.

And now, flickering strips of the frailest gold leaf – like hard-won tribute – are laid out before each one of them on an expansively silken, ruffled sea, as if apportioning forgiveness, granting them leave to soften at last. How this morning seems to succour them, as if ministering all manner of comfort to them, as if God

3

has finally relented, is finally resting their souls. This time, the dawn has brought with it a dream, and not its forsaking...

For an hour or so, they are a dot in bliss, idling in the early sun, the world held off in a great abeyance. The outline of a coast gradually establishes itself. The whole idea of Italy, which has sustained them for so long, starts to come true in a thin, dissolving haze, there, on the horizon. As the pitch-blue softens, they know the worst of the sea is properly behind them, will soon be forgotten. And though the voyage has done its damage, coarsening them, showing them the little they have and are, has exacted from them whatever it wanted, whenever it wanted, – terrible, weak vows made supine or turned away on their sides – here they are, the four of them, out on deck, twirling about as if at a fair, happy at last with what they're seeing.

Nature, for once on her best behaviour, seems determined not to let them down: unlike those other heaped, squat ports they've seen in the distance, those reluctant harbours cagily tensed at the periphery of things, the curve of the bay simply encourages them in. They watch as it slowly unsheathes its blade, unaware of how close they've got to each other. Out come the glints, dazzling them completely. Straight away, their hands go up to shield their eyes. None of them has ever seen the like before, not remotely the like, not even the two gentlemen. All around them, the blue blazes...

4

Who would be the first to close his eyes on this? All four of them just stand there, craning into the east, lapped at by the light, watching it fatten through their fingers, like watching glass blown. Severn, who can never keep still, looks for a moment positively beatific, rapt; sun-struck and brim-full, he's already raised his arms, as if about to lead some applause. He can feel another of his rhapsodic episodes coming on. Italy! O Italy! What can't a man achieve now? Severn looks and looks again, for all he's worth. These particular colours must be got by heart, for the bay, the land and all their futures in them, can only bring them good.

Mrs Pidgeon, meanwhile, simply keeps her poise, watching over Miss Cotterell, steadying her, in case she starts to expect too much. A good part of her would like to join Mr Severn in his marvelling, despite all that's grown between them. The light's now surely sweet enough to smooth away their differences. In truth, she hasn't stopped thinking about the night of the storm, the one that nearly undid her, had her scrabbling at anyone who came near. The way Severn holds his hands out, pawing at the air as if to catch it, is enough to remind her. She came apart like a cracked old soap in its dish. Utterly useless, everything she'd held dear up to that point. Nothing to do about it but take the steps she'd taken, of course. She'd had to hide it, afterwards, give herself over to a studied, cold resolve. Not much appetite, thereafter, to sit beside the chastened Miss

5

Cotterell and administer and pander to her, her own fellow-feeling rimed and crusted hard, like a barrelful of salted pork. Deep down, she just wants to be where no pleading voice can reach her. She knows she said too much that time, when the girl was in mortal danger, made herself too plain. From then on, she knew, there'd be no more sitting to brush the girl's fair hair out for her, no more plaiting and tying on of ribbons, murmuring lines from this year's songs. She feels it well up in her all over again, making her hot. She feels her face redden.

She was right to keep silent.

Severn suddenly dashes off to the starboard side to get another perspective. Miss Cotterell follows him with her eyes. When he straightens up like that, filling himself with the best of the light, surely he looks just like her brother must, if only she could remember him... Of course she's fond of Mr Severn, but it's Mr Keats she wants to hear from. But she mustn't press him. In any case, she wouldn't mind being left like this a little while longer, the whole bay held up for them in a toast to health and happiness, like Apollo's golden cup, gleaming and inviting them – why not? She deserves it, they all do! – to drink their fill. What seemed a moment ago to be so unlikely, trembling on the edge of what God makes possible, now reveals itself in its spectacular sweep. As far as she's concerned, it's a glittering bowl of rose-water, nothing less. Or maybe a gilded punchbowl for water-nymphs to tumble in. Rather pleased with

6

this, she smiles, her lips held out as if awaiting a first sip. A pretty kiss. The whitest fingertips.

'See, Mr Keats,' she finally calls out. 'There's your answer, right there before you now.'

In time, Keats thinks, all spells are broken. He shakes his head and blinks, as if coming to, would like to pretend he hasn't heard her. His eyes are still swimming. Besides, Miss Cotterell wouldn't really want to hear what he's been thinking, that all this has come too late for them. And if he can't say such a thing, why say anything? Once again, she's managed to annoy him. It seems like none of them will leave him be. Yet what she says is true enough: Nature has – incredibly – provided. Any fool can see that. Which means he can't be as far gone as he supposed: the world still reaches him, still has its effect on him, still, for whatever reason, matters. But why, after all it's done to him, would it rear up all of a sudden like this, to catch him off guard completely?

'I say, Mr Keats!'

Her voice comes at him again. To show her he's heard, he holds one hand up, then leans his elbow against the rail to brace himself for talk. The invalid creakily turns himself around. In a moment, he will have to engage with her, but not just yet. His illness has its uses. What he really wants is to stay right here, within himself; of course he does, doesn't everyone? Even Severn over there. But this morning, he must admit, it does seem as if joy, patched and bandaged and barely

7

recognisable, but joy nonetheless, has in fact caught up with him. Yes, joy, joy, of all things, pierces him through and through. *Come to me, come to me*, its poor thin arms seem to say, held out as wide as any hostage's. He longs to follow, but knows that if he does, it will bring an unenviable estrangement. Who would he even be, these past few months, without all of dying's certainties, its clear-eyed sufferings? He's felt – and thought of – little else since summer, more used now to the bouts of self-hate, to the pangs and the delirium, the shaming loss of self-control. He knows what he's pretending not to: the raging soreness in his throat, the raking cough he can never shake off, the constant fear of a haemorrhage, the gouts of spittle and blood. Any improvements he makes, a spell of calm or mere indifference, he's learned to consider temporary, slim. Experience tells him so. The entire voyage a lesson in this, got by heart, a lesson repeatedly shouted into his face, the strap raised, his only response a trembling chalk-scrape on his slate, a schoolboy's cowering question for the master.

'What do you have to say to that, I wonder?'

He looks across at Miss Cotterell, drawn to the tight sound of triumph in her voice. He knows too well her tell-tale, sallow skin, her scaly, crabbed hands which fret at themselves, her stooped stick-shoulders that shake with too much expressiveness of one kind or another. Her gaiety borrows heavily from despair. As if she were trying to overcome some back-stage nerves, by seeming

8

bold. Throughout the trip, they have matched each other crisis for crisis, running high fevers against each other, alternating fits of coughing, nights of retching and fainting, as if caught up in the competitiveness of a stupid race – who can hold their breath and stay down longer? They regard each other sometimes with the fierceness of respect. If one had scars, the other would no doubt be eyeing them jealously. What a sorry, delicate, disgruntled pair they've made, conniving at each other's agonies, vying all journey, each one aiming to outlast the other. And she, always with her God beside her, helping her to stave off death.

She has turned to face him fully now, and what he sees takes him unawares. She's never looked so expansive. Her whole being flares out; the newly-raised flag of herself flaps its unlikely flush of colour in the breeze.

'Look, Mr Keats, look!'

'I assure you, Miss Cotterell, I do, I do.'

'But can't you see, it's all around us, the sky...the sea...' she starts to explain, flourishing a dainty hand at the distance to help her finish her sentence. All this is ours, her gesture says, has lain in wait for us, even in our worst hours, when we thought... She continues to point proudly, vaguely, as if the bay's magical, gradual unfolding were secretly, and all along, down to her. As if any one of them could have conjured the succession of cliffs and coves, variations of sheer and sloping, sacred

9

and sublime. She radiates so much hope, it's as if some transforming power had poured pure zeal inside her. She could be Danae under her sunburst of ravishing gold; well, she almost could be. Ah, to be able to believe like that, to be at once the charmed and anointed one, the enchantress stumbling about her rooms in the bright hours, drunk with conviction, clutching the bottle and tasting the elixir. Those bitter-sweet drops. She can tell she has his attention, his eyes unusually large and sympathetic.

'What I mean to say is...' She realizes she's being breathless and sees to it at once. Her hand goes across her heart, as if to relieve it, then up to her throat.

'Is it not in every last detail what I described to you?' she continues, more measured now. 'Didn't I say there'd be sights worth seeing? Didn't we all promise ourselves pleasures like this?'

Why not warm to her? She looks as heartfelt as she sounds. He knows all about her loneliness, and something of her longings: women, too, cry out in their sleep. Is she not, in her own way, a paragon of sorts? Her ability to get this far seems to him more commendable than his own base groping after patience.

'We might well have said something of the kind,' he smiles back.

It must be safe now, at trials' end, for the two of them to exchange kind glances, without being misinterpreted. Now she's got where she wanted, he imagines she feels

10

she can gush all she likes. Her reunion with her brother can be only a matter of hours away.

'You see. It seems fate after all does care for you and your kind.'

In another world, in other circumstances, Keats thinks, she would be considered charming and desirable, working her eyelashes like that; he can picture her angling her cheek, sending out hint-heavy words from behind an astute fan.

'You're right. It is exactly as you wished, Miss Cotterell. The bay, the view, all of it finer than any of us could have wished.'

A blonde tress has come loose; she should fix that behind her ear, but she hasn't noticed. Many men would have willingly done their best for her, if she'd been given the chance to make them.

'If you've felt what I have in any way – as you must – you'll have wished for this with all your soul. If heaven can't compare to this, or something very like it, then heaven's not...'

'Heaven?' he interrupts. 'You're getting ahead of yourself, I hope, Miss Cotterell. I don't think any of us intended to pay a visit there on our voyage out.'

It appears Miss Cotterell's spiritedness is mostly down to the spiritual. A shame. Mawkishness dressed as sermonising – save him from a schoolgirl's piety. Fearing an outpouring, Keats turns to the sun, crinkling his face, his eyelids pursing in the brightness, as if

11

wincing at a lapse in her. Let that look answer for him. But Miss Cotterell's seen nothing amiss.

'And our other wishes,' she goes on, unaware that she's leant her forehead closer to him, her shadow overlapping his, 'you'll concede, might also now come true? That endings can be happy too?'

The vertical frown lines shoot up in alarm; he feels hemmed in, forced to look at her more carefully now. God save him from a revelation, a last-minute, now-the-coast-is-clear conversion. She's far more robust than he'd thought.

'Regrettably, our hearts cannot yet command where we would wish. At least, not to *our* recollection.' He turns deliberately, though wishing no snub to her, over to where Severn stands, still sea-gazing, in need right now of one of his interventions: 'Isn't that so, Mr Severn?'

Severn duly turns round. 'Isn't what so?'

'Miss Cotterell was asking whether we had much say on our future happiness.'

'Why, Miss Cotterell, of course! In scenes like these,' and he makes the very same gesture that she had made, waving at the blue, 'how could a man fail to believe...'

Severn's descriptive powers get underway, with gusto. Keats is guiltily relieved. He discreetly mops at his temples, wiping finger-tips of sweat in his palms, feeling his forebodings coming back. This fencing tires him; he really shouldn't engage. He's halt and

12

parries without conviction. There's always someone, some acquaintance or other, stealing the prospect, shouldering in, standing too close or simply in more of the light, someone who's only too happy to tell him what to feel and when, someone who'll keep on at him till he gives them his accord. Why can't others watch what they're saying? Their truisms are as welcome as stones, as chill as cleverness. Better to be on his own. Far better. Trying to look unconcerned, he gets up to cede his place to Severn and wanders off, feeling the sun full on him.

For a long while, he stays like this, his hands at rest on the rail, approving of every hidden inlet as they come clear for him, wresting the detail, taking it in, saving it for another time, when time might be less exacting. He could watch all day the luminous, fraught sparring of rock and swell, listen to the whump of the big waves – perpetually renewed – how they end in a hiss of high-flung spray.

Eventually, the rhythm of the distant boom and the ceaseless dashing tires him. He supposes he should sit back down, but Severn and the girl are still gamely at their talking. The sun is fiercer now. He turns to contemplate it, to wonder yet again how it's meant to save him, do him good. He knows he must be careful. If he looks too long, its rays will angle into him, searching him for weakness, for the moment when his eyes give in. Light like this can make a man see too clearly into things. His case is hopeless, after all. An arrow, sharpened and barbed with a merciless glitter, has been sent to single him out, to fix him there and define him as some solitary, unfit wanderer, forever. He did not ask to be chosen; he feels his resolve beginning to fail. This is where he ends, isn't it? Under a hostile sun, scrutinised till he burns and writhes. He has no chance of leaving this coast. He scarcely has the strength to make it ashore, never mind the onward leg of the journey inland. Rome's a mirage, a lure, false bait and fable. Gold flares into his eyes till it wrings a sharp cry from him. Brilliant red flashes ignite behind his lids, in a wicked conflagration. More sounds escape him; injudicious moans. He hears Severn's words - 'Not necessarily. Keats, for instance, is hardly the sort to bel...' - abruptly cut away, as if he's sensed something's wrong. Keats is struggling to keep his balance and is barely aware of it, is floundering across the deck, like Saul, recoiling from the truth. For a man who has lived so long in his mind, drinking in impressions, encouraging fancy, this clarity comes as a physical blow, a cleaving.

Severn is instantly there, catching him under the arms, holding him steady. That a man should feel so light, scarcely the meat of a proper carcase on him... Keats' breaths come in short, hard gasps. He babbles the start of an apology, then holds his tongue, chewing on his humiliation like a famished dog when it gets its bone thrown back. He manages to crumple into his chair, hunched into a caricature of himself as an idiot, keeping

14

his head thrust down, his jaw still working, hissing and spitting as Severn takes charge. The pains go through and through him, until the bout passes. When he can finally speak again, he mutters,

'Is everyone to stand about and see me like this...?'

Through all this, Miss Cotterell's hands cover her mouth, but can't prevent what's coming out; little, breathy yelps of anguished fellow-feeling. To see him like this, when but a minute ago... She knows her stupidly standing there only makes things worse, but can't stop looking at him, repelled and curious and terribly crestfallen. She hears every word of what he's saying. Now everything is ruined. Since there's no one else, she takes her distress straight to Mrs Pidgeon, who says she didn't see a thing.

'Come here, child, with me,' she counsels, 'out of harm's way.'

She puts an arm round the girl's tiny shoulders, presses her heavy head down against her heart.

'Don't let it upset you so.'

For someone usually so dependably impassive, rigid enough to stand in for a figurehead, Mrs Pidgeon's somewhat surprised at herself, her own voice wavering with emotion. The end in sight has flustered them all. With something approaching good grace, she lends the girl her arm, and sets about steeling her once more.

Left alone in all that empty blue, Severn has somehow managed to calm Keats down. The fever has

15

gone; his cough has subsided; his pulse has slowed to normal, more or less. The two of them look down at what Keats has been spitting out: fortunately, no blood this time.

'It's all right, it's all right,' Severn murmurs, like his mother used to do, cradling his friend's head, stroking his back, as the first of the sobs work through him.

Part Two

The River

London, September 1820

A stroll down Fleet Street

Holed up since Wednesday at Taylor's, Keats has gloomed through the days, struggling to appear grateful, feeling oily and exhausted. He sleeps through as many hours as he can. There's been some unforeseen delay over the ship; nothing's ready, nothing is made easy for him. And since he daren't go back to Hampstead, to the woman he loves, instead he mopes and flickers through strange rooms uncertainly, his fingers trailing along tables cluttered with books and papers and unrestrained begging letters.

Taylor is often out on publisher's business, but friends call by as if by chance and try to rouse him; he's never felt so well-acquainted, so bereft. Yes, it's a great

17

shame he's leaving, yes, London's never looked finer, yes, he is thinking of another book, yes, it will be all about love again. The old set: a tense line of well-wishers he has to play out, keep at arms' length with a range of courtesies, well-placed hums and haws. They can't quite bring themselves to say what they've come to say; Keats bows and does his share of smiling and throughout it all, he suffers their curiosity, getting up now and again to stir at an ashy fire, poking at it forcibly, dashing the embers to pieces. Yes, he understands, yes, he ought to be more...

In quiet hours, Taylor's library solves nothing; there's no courage to be had in a book. Nothing for him in any of the leaves he turns over, all the while hating himself for not going back to his fiancee. Yet he knows he can't. Unendurable, the invalid's abashed return, meekly unlatching the wicket-gate, seeing white faces in the windows. The instinctive shrug of his shoulders; *sorry, so sorry, but I've had to come back.* Needlessly cruel, another round of wordless goodbyes, the loved mouths opening and closing, their pitying eyes to look long into all over again. Above all, have the heart, the fortitude, to spare her that. He taps a few spines, drumming lacklustre fingers, and then goes over to the window. The wise man must look within himself. All Keats does is to pick at himself like a sore. He needs to get out, needs to get some other air, even if it's London air. He should call in on Dilke, over at Somerset House,

18

while he's about it. That recent disagreement of theirs surely can be straightened out; he has the time, clearly, and making amends still seems worthwhile.

Unnoticed, he lets himself out into the street, carefully, pulling on gloves, wrapped against the city's wiles. Out there, it's mayhem. As soon as he turns round, still on the first step, he has to take that deep, startled breath, as if he'd locked himself out or left something important behind. But it's nothing to do with him or how he feels. It's simply London that takes him by surprise, London that surges straight at him, snarling and hurling itself at him, pitching in to him with its menacing, brute free-for-all. Its noise is instantly onto him, sensing him falter there, his hand guarding his throat, and it pins him back to the wall, like a mad old woman screaming herself vengeful and hoarse.

Thus the world barrels on, ready to square up to anyone – anyone different or shifty or weak. Up and down, in either direction, the long livid street issues its bare-knuckle challenge: *Live with this, if you can.* And so John Keats steps out to answer it, just as he's always done.

For a full two hundred and fifty yards he manages. Swirled along, jostled and cursed at like an invalid, he does his best to keep out of the current, knowing he'd see the dangers too late. Shallows are everywhere. 'Hey, you, you weren't even looking!' And judging by the resentment he gets – the tuts and frowns, one

19

great elbow to the cheek – he must look a downright dissolute, dangerously irresolute in a greatcoat that can't possibly be his. The number of times he's forced to make way. Forced like the worst of men to trawl in the shadows, feeling grimed and risible, fallible, some faltering guttersnipe, some muttering lowlife type of whom everyone suspects the worst. He has to stop and think. Put a sudden stop to this stubbornness of his. He takes the first side street that offers itself and rights himself by some railings, holding on to some metal fleur-de-lys, thoroughly winded, scooped out. He already had a sore throat he couldn't quite clear. Now that tenderness under his arms is back. Sweat pricks his scalp. He wipes his palms several times on his trousers. What is he doing here?

Almost shorn of purpose, he hunkers down on a scorched stone step, where a sparrow flits, and reaches for his watch. How much longer till Sunday? More hours than he'd hoped to put up with. What now? Shouldn't he just head back? But then there'd be all that ado, explanations. He can't bear the faces anxiety makes. If he heads for Covent Garden, he could buy a bag of apples, or pastries, watch things happen. Somewhere round here, there's a gateway to the Inner Temple where well-tended greens stretch peaceably down to the river. But he won't go there now. Nor can he stay here for long; people are quick to get angry; crowds soon draw near. The last thing he wants is attention. He still hasn't said

20

sorry to Dilke. Thinking of this, he's suddenly conscious of someone under his shoulder looking up at him through the bars and smudges of a basement window. A girl of three or four, well-dressed, her fair hair in braids, seems to have just stopped singing, her mouth is rounded so. She holds a wooden toy in her hands and spins its red wheels. She peers up at his funny face with a mix of sawing curiosity and alarm. She moves her hand towards her mouth. Don't be scared, he thinks. Don't be scared of the pinched, little man. His song is nearly done. God forbid he should spoil her play. He labours to his feet and to reassure her, makes a show of dusting himself down. When he looks back, she's no longer there.

Since there's nothing for it but Fleet Street again, he ducks back into the press and flow. The city, he finds, once his panic has gone, soon pays him no attention, goes on spoiling its already spoilt self, pouring out its arguments, its cries and confusions, its hectic spectacle, its heavy mean thrum. As he settles to a tolerable, sensible pace, he sees an Empire's rich pickings being peddled around him. Everyone, it seems, is out for something, something obvious, mostly pleasures and gain. Maidservants and loungers, strollers and errand-boys, loiterers and law-abiders, idiots, idlers. They all clump along merrily or moodily enough. When he stops for a rest outside a baker's, he listens to the continuous vying drone; gull-faced porters grunting and muttering,

21

their barrows spilling with greens; a swarthy man doing nothing but shout ostentatiously, his voice a fob watch held up to the light; two gangly coves being sick together in a dark spot; a group of stalwart ladies blinking back the shock. And there's plenty more: two or three wiry lawyers deep in new jargon; pie-hawkers; lots of rich Dutch; tripe-friers too; hustlers and odd-jobbers; a group of sparks spilled out from a coffee-house, swapping larks; a rank shellfish stall where a tomcat eyes his chance; a bored harlot picking her nose, her black fan limp in her other hand; and, over there, before an impressive front, a brisk melee, followed by some scoundrel running off.

Under it all – can't they feel it? – a sense of a candle flame being slowly extinguished, a pinch of sooty fingers menacing. The shadows are coming. *Tired of London, tired of life.* He feels the full force of the famous phrase, and more; feels terrified. What's happened to him? Didn't he once wear the world like a bauble, extravagantly taking his time? Out and about like one in a gallows-crowd, enjoying his holiday? He used to love having time on his hands more than anyone he knew...

Not so long ago, a day's freedom was enough to send a young man into raptures. He thinks about that time, three years ago now, when he went bounding off to the Vale of Health on a day like this, a sheaf of new sonnets tucked safe in his jacket pocket, off to meet his idol, Liberty's champion, the poet and radical Leigh

22

Hunt, released that summer from prison. With Spring in his every step, getting good lines from Spenser by heart, he saw nothing much about him, Autumn reduced to a blurred, golden backdrop. London receded meekly, in a straggle of cottages and abundant market gardens. Loose leaves were falling, strewing themselves at his feet. He was listening out for the whispers of fame. Loftily he strode on, dream-driven, thinking of Hunt's inner circle, of a fellowship of like minds. How would they treat him? What share of the glory would be his? What would he prefer – advice or acclaim? Plain, just words from the already-published? He felt his vocation stir within him; here he was, escaped at last from the apothecary's drudgery, taking his first real steps on his own, rehearsing his goodbye to Guy's – all his medical training, the fees invested in him. Good riddance to good sense. No one knew what he had in him. His big heart filled with blood, promise. Words winged him up and down lanes, shaping him truly, filling him out; he felt strange to himself, wondering, yielding; it felt like he was scrambling up Parnassus, trying to prove himself fitter than the others. Where had Charles got to? He was supposed to be making the introductions! Couldn't he keep up? There he was, a hundred yards behind, toiling now into view, thoroughly puffed and miffed. He said he'd been calling him for the past mile and a half. Acclaim's echo urging Keats on! What a welcome he'd receive! What a coronation! Such early boy-promise...

23

Dilke is not at his office. No, it was of no real importance. He would call again, another time. He declines a cup of tea, declines to leave a message. He pulls the door to behind him, fumbling for his breath. He ought to keep moving. The cold is getting back into his hands. For a minute, he lingers by a window, but what he sees of the river - glum and hostile and spiny with masts – fails to console him. He feels more and more deterred, shabbier, moth-eaten, labouring down the last set of stairs, out into the courtyard of Somerset House, whose absolute symmetry, full of needless embellishments – arches, pediments, reliefs – subdues him, freights his shoulders with yet more dissatisfaction. He picks his way across the cobbles, diminished, a down-at-heel, berating his bad luck, a beggar bent over, machinating. Others, in more stylish, well-polished shoes, subtly steer clear of him. He could be any disgruntled seaman, paying his lack of respect to the Admiralty. Distracted, he flinches from the nervous flutter of three or four pigeons that seem to have deliberately targeted him, making him flap out a hand, weakly, shooing them off. Plainly, this courtyard has no place for the likes of him. When he reaches the magnificent entrance arch and senses what awaits him out there – more and more ordeal – he's not sure what's to blame, whether it's the bells of St. Mary's ringing out three and not four, or the clacking of dispirited hooves, or the tumbril-scrape of unrelenting wheels – all manner of carriages and wagons

24

and handcarts hurrying on, grating iron on stone - but whatever the cause, there, in a sudden lunge of light, he feels stricken, forsaken, forced by circumstance to look directly at something he'd rather not. And it's now, when there's nothing he wants from this world any more, when he's done with the costing, the haggling, the airy just-looking, it's now that Keats sees what he's privately wished for all summer: the democracy of affliction.

At last, everyone else can be made to feel what he's been going through. If he keeps his eyes closed long enough, he can see the whole of Fleet Street and The Strand laid bare, its traffic stalled and seized with a paralysis, everyone struck down, laid low by a hundred time-honoured diseases, by old-age's abominations, by a breviary of plagues. Pain's gamut runs down the road, indiscriminately, levelling them all, leaving passers-by clutching at stomachs and heads, as if enacting horrors, their drawn mouths stuffed with the taste of unwanted last words. Some fall to their knees, furious with themselves; some fold over, simply disappointed; some writhe, drawing out their throes, too caught up in their agonies to care how they look. It's a vision straight out of Revelations, or Bosch; bad scenes from the operating theatre at Guy's; screams he's not had to hear in years. All sorts of men and women, finding themselves repulsive at last, dab frantically at ulcers and cancres, buboes and goitres; gouty sophisticates stumble as if through fire; palsied greybeards call out in their misery, gripping

25

onto railings, their death-rattles gradually choked off; old maids collapse in attitudes of incomprehension; flesh-wounds fester on penitent redcoats; new strains of syphilis make the sinful gibber; both great and small poxes blossom like elderflowers; everywhere, tumbling from horses and carriages onto gutters and pavements made slippery with vomit and dysentry, there are victims brandishing superb inflammations, neck-boils the size of babies' heads continuously seeping... The damned made to dance their conspicuous come-uppance.

Keats feels nothing, watching his imagination at work. Strange, in a world so murderously taken up with itself, that there's so little blood.

'What in God's name is keeping him?' Haslam wants to know. Severn is late, as usual. Keats half-expects he's changed his mind and wouldn't hold it against him: what kind of man would volunteer to be Death's assistant? Amenuensis mori. The faithful companion has grown rather unfashionable of late, he's noticed. Which might explain why normally steadfast men like Haslam and Woodhouse can be so peacock-headed, so agitated and gnawed upon, clucking and strutting on the quayside like leading players at the operetta. Why are they all so on edge? Everything is irrevocable now. It's the guilt at not coming with him, he supposes, it's the vacancy at the heart of things. Should something be wrong, Keats would be the most relieved of them all, happy to have his decisions taken from him, his half-hopes dashed, his last winter delivered up in a familiar Hampstead bed under the eyes of those who love him, with the consolation of one last reunion.

'Patience, Haslam. You should take your cue from Taylor here. A good publisher never rushes an artist.'

Taylor smiles indulgently, but he shares Haslam's alarm. Any sensible man would think twice before attempting the Atlantic this late in the season with nothing more to look forward to than nursing a dying man. And Severn's no fool. Could he be reconsidering even now? A scapegoat messenger could arrive any minute bringing a perfectly acceptable apology. By his own account, the man has no stomach for the sea, nor has he been in the best of health for weeks. And Biscay is not for beginners. You don't push a weak swimmer off a rowboat in the middle of a lake and ask him to make for shore.

'He'd have sent word if he couldn't come,' Keats adds. 'He's always been a man of his word.'

The three men turn as one, as if conscience-pricked, but Keats broadens his smile, has clearly meant nothing untoward by this. Keats himself sits tight in his sullen boots, his back against a bollard, bony hands pressing into bony knees, a remote, morose imitation of calm. Quite out of character, unless this tense, clamped shell is to be the final version of him. By rights, he should be the one pacing about, red-faced and overreacting, visibly strained and altered into discomposure's posturings, like a famished fowl flushed out of cover, shrieking at the conniving air, hearing gunshots. His friends are too kind in their indignation, spitting out feathers on his behalf.

Keats pats his pockets to pass the time. About him, he knows full well, are his secrets; his last wishes, relics that no one shall prise from him, kept in the lining of his coat. He's been a clever little stowaway: he can feel against his ribs the marble cornelian; the pocketbook with something in her hand. Whilst the others fret at the advancing tide, he treats himself to a private smile: he's got Melancholy's trophies all to himself.

28

Meanwhile, all around him, nothing but omens. The clouds haven't changed for one minute, weighty and unmoving, irrefutably gloomy. Not a chance of sunlight to nurse himself in. All the evidence points to a curse on him and his loved ones, a fatal design marking them out from the beginning, something Greek and malign. He might as well be bound for Troy. Woodhouse, anxious for a lock of the poet's hair, puffs his cheeks ponderously like an over-applauded Kean, and keeps on quipping, furiously. Haslam laughs too loud at everything. The two of them, Keats can tell, are wanting to say something kind and valuable, memorable, but don't know how to begin. The muteness of Keats' look, his shame at still being sick make anything but the knife-grinding of goodbye difficult to talk about. To strike up conversation, his friends have to pick their way through a maze of possible indelicacies – merely mentioning the coming London theatre season, autumn on the Heath, another poet's forthcoming volume, tiresome office snags, the best teacakes in the Strand, the pleasures of the fireside hearth, what's in the latest *Examiner*, could cause offence. And God forbid a scene, a moment of lost resolve out here. Best to leave him be, crouching there on the cobblestones, scarcely bothering to look up. A luckless let-down lark without its song, its instinctive upwards hurl and trill, for now, at least, quite gone.

As they wait, yet more carriages draw up to set down numbed or flustered passengers who, one by one, duck into the dun fug of Thames-side air, rubbing their eyes and stretching their legs, beginning to wonder at their circumstances. They loiter, looking lost and suddenly slack, like coils of rope round a redundant barrel. What can they make of it all? Some of them cast about greedily, taking in the new and magnificent; others must have much further still to go. Wherever they look, getting their bearings, the impassive Tower rises above them, with its grey, sobering stone seeing in a grey, sobering Sunday. A day of rest, a good day to sink to your knees and repent. And everywhere, wheeling insatiable gulls, plaintive and unnerving, mocking Keats' crabbed attempt at insouciance.

By now, he is completely out of disguises, seriously sour-faced, transparent. *Leave me and my ruin in peace* his jaw line threatens. His determinedly dry eyes won't focus on the reunions going on all around him, with their repetitive motifs of stupor and relief - huddling families so breathlessly happy their bodies shake, as though in convulsions; couples halted, still yards apart, rooted to the ground in rapt recognition, their hands going up to their open mouths. All this, as if to spite or bait him.

Finally, there's a faint disturbance over by the inn, a ripple of something desperate and earnest, and they make out Severn pushing past some onlookers, a stumbling uncertain angel come to announce what kept him. He is the very devil of dishevelment, a blond

30

bewilderment of unswept hair, a French king's ransom of curls, proffering his excuses. Ah. There will be no reprieve, no trudge homewards, after all. His friends rush over. Severn appears moved. Keats could do with helping up, could do with a hold full of ballast to steady him now, but gets to his feet while their backs are turned and manages to stand, as if to some half-remembered attention. His hand, when Severn clasps it, is unexpectedly cold. Keats grins.

'What are we waiting for, gentlemen?'

He lets them go ahead, intending to stay a while longer, to feel his goodbyes, but there's suddenly too much to take in.

31

Settled

That morning, Severn felt awful, under-slept, the whole mad project, his reckless charity, preying on his mind. He'd be putting to sea in less than six hours. All the second thoughts imaginable were with him, jostling him, ribbing him, whispering, *Why did you accept? How well do you really know him, this Keats?* At the washbasin, groggily, puffily under-prepared, he watched the water sluice through his fingers. Try again. He stared at the hairline crack in the porcelain. When he steeped his hands in the cool, he felt nothing but lukewarm spreading its way up. He'd run himself rheumy lately, exhausted himself with his energy. What a seven days' palaver. The hands he'd shaken, the debts he'd called in, the friends he'd had to embrace. He groped for the hand towel, hoping to ruffle his tiredness away, but emerged more shock-headed than ever, with a lunatic's wry smile.

When he stepped back to look round his room, he couldn't get his bearings; emptied of almost everything that made him who he is, it gave him a blank look back, in all innocence, like a stripped theatre set caught between acts. Was this all there was to him – a box of his first attempts at sketches and a pile of books he'd outgrown huddled against a wall?

He dressed quickly, checked his pockets – those vital introductions for Rome – and listened at the door. He could hear his sister rustling in the hallway, waiting

32

for him. When they embraced, his weak goodbye came out as a whisper. He kept his eyes closed, whilst she said nothing. His heart was racing, running away, a high-seas adventurer. And that was the easy, loving-tender part, shearing off from her lovely eyes as she held onto him for a moment longer; it's what waited in Shoreditch, at the family home, that was making him blanch. Father. The last thing he wanted was a fit of accusations and having to listen yet again to his own explanations. Their philosophies were at breaking point. The son was making his rash, uncertain way in the world, the way sons had always done. And that was that. Surely. He nodded to the driver's expressionless face, who duly flicked the reins. Off into the morning dark.

When his mother answered his knock at once, he started to fear the worst. She loved him with all her heart but then he knew that, didn't he? Yes, mother, yes, but he wasn't thinking of that. Unfortunately, his own head was in disarray, cluttered with memories of other difficult leave-takings – proper ruptures – he'd managed to keep from surfacing, till now; unpleasant scenes full of his bravado pressed in on him, moments when he should have stood his ground; failed responsibilities to his friends, urgent letters he should have written; unresolved financial matters. All of this detritus leaving little room for Rome, for the dream-scent of pines on the Palatine Hill; grave thoughts in the Forum; the sheer drop at the Tarpeian rock; idle, skinny boys throwing

33

stones at the Tiber; the thrill of seeing the Laocoon.

She hurried him through, pulling on his sleeve. He really *was* running away, then. He could see his father's knuckles whitening round his cane, could feel the unease, nestling in his spine. Though of course he was spineless, senseless, a child still not ready for his breeches. In the kitchen, all of his mother's fondness, all her fears for him were apparent in the piled plate of bread and butter and jam she'd laid out for him, knowing he'd be hungry. Between huge mouthfuls, as she stood watching over him, he could hear his bull-father in the drawing room, rancorous and defeated. He wouldn't look up at her. Since Severn, the eldest, had found his own direction, that man hurled himself at whatever tried to go from him – whether health or children or the remains of happiness. He stubbed himself out, kicking at furniture, madding himself into a misery so deep no one wanted to go near him, help pull him out. Severn recalled the baiting he'd received only too well. He wiped at his mouth; best to get it over with, this defiance of the father who gave him everything, yet understood nothing.

In his green armchair, his father looked as absurd and as ragged as a plucked hen. His neck was rubbed horribly red and distended. Some bitter pleasure about to be taken pulsed in him. His furtive eyes jerked up when he sensed Severn come in. He looked like he'd seen a snake and would scotch it. Regardless, Severn

34

stepped into the four square panes of first light from the big sash-window, and forced the old man's hand.

'I take it you've called by to tell me you've changed your mind?'

Severn said nothing.

'Why else take up my time?'

'Sir, as I have explained, Rome will be a...'

'Rome? Rome? Is that your answer to everything? Deserting your mother for the sake of a whim? Building your dreams on plans without foundations? Ignoring good advice?'

His father struggled to his feet, wanting his contorting face thrust as uncomfortably close as he could get it to make his son take a step back.

'Come for my blessing, have you? A blessing you'll never get?'

Severn chanced a nod, still hoping to diffuse the old man.

'Speak up boy, I can't hear you, I can't understand you. It's years since I did. Think you can go off in the brave wide world without my permission? Employ your mother against me? Pleading with me over and over on your behalf? Is that what you think?'

'Sir, I must...' Severn took the necessary steps back, trying to accept the rebuke, but his distress only encouraged his father.

'Hoping no doubt,' – at this point, all decorum lost, his father prodded Severn's chest – 'to make off while an old man's back is turned? A man who's always known where his rightful place is, where his duty to others lies? You'd stoop to this, a coward's trick, would you?'

The blow, when it came, came as no surprise, though it knocked Severn to the floor. He saw the old man hesitate, as if remembering what to do, how to strike his own. He saw the fist clenching purposefully, the liver-spots patterning the skin, the white cuffs sliding back down the wilful, trembling white-haired arm. All along, he thought his father would think better of it. There is a divide that few men, even one as unhappy as his father, are willing to cross, knowing it means irrecoverable distance, the public shame of an unnatural breach. Bloodshed as watershed. Severn flinched too late, heard himself cry out, girlishly, having no answer to ire as pure as this. To have his own forbidding, loving father rain down blows on him? In what way had he deserved it? What had he ever done wrong, except be his son?

He was caught on the temple and down he went, a crumpled, scandalized thing. Add weak-kneed to his other failings. His right elbow rucked several folds into the rug, his left forearm held up in vain, fending off the weight of twelve years or more of failed expectations. His mother must have called out, too, for his brother bounded in, instantly alert, knowing what to do, primed to hold his father back. For several seconds, nothing – neither the outrage nor the hurt – abated in the least. He kept expecting the worn old man to look suddenly

36

aghast, to break up against the hard fact of his leaving, give way wholly to an access of remorse. Instead, his brother wrestled his father down, face to ghastly face, their teeth fixed in terrible grins.

Severn had to pick himself up in a hurry, his soles slipping on the floor. In his gathering fury and shame, he bolted from his mother's pity, knocking her hand away, staggered instinctively back the way he came, towards the front door, fiddling at the damned locks, blundering out into the street. When he finally turned round, stilling the urge to run on down the empty futile street, fighting off tears, he took in the whole hostile facade of the house up as far as his old bedroom window and saw, finally, how he'd outgrown it. No wild faces appeared at the windows downstairs; the scuffles had died down. Quiet dawn in the street; the horse's stamping. Severn felt his jaw. He had to go on straightening himself for some time, vowing and cursing and disbelieving, until his brother came out.

'Let's walk a little. He says he won't make his peace. Mother will be fine; she knows how to be with him. There's no question of me not coming with you now, at least as far as the river. When you're ready, that is.'

Severn looked past him.

'Joseph, there's nothing for you here.'

A shrug was all he allowed himself, before the two of them made off, quickening their pace, like ghosts set on a haunting, his younger brother's arm around him.

37

Their heads leaned together, as if conspiring. Patricide on Severn's mind. Only when he had properly cooled, having walked to the crossroads and back several times, and had promised he'd write, did they return to the house. Severn stepped straight into the cab. Staring ahead at the disappointments of another day, the driver showed nothing, not even the thin, patient smile of the man promised money, waiting for another nod from the gentleman.

'No, you're right. That settles everything,' Severn said.

Uncompanionable

When Keats takes those seven steps down to the cabin, refusing to feel anything, he knows he has entered another, very different room, his last parlour, a far chamber, obscure and subdued, where a charmless woman-in-waiting waits, obliging with a stirred pot of black tea and little obvious warmth. The spoon tinkles against the rim of the pot. He feels her measuring him up. Even in a light as poor and unassuming as this, she wears her suspicion in her face. Or maybe fears. How much has she been told? She looks strangely at home already, grey and dimmed as though, a long time ago, she was ordered down here and made to grow old, forgotten by the world above, and had dowdily made do ever since.

'How long have you been in here?' he struggles to say, as though she were something out of Dante. This woman - he's sure of it, the way she holds his gaze - will be his Charon, his matronly Virgil, poling him through the sulphur and the gloom. Does that smile of hers understand him? Will he be obliged to look to her for sympathy? For now, it's enough that she pours him out a cup. A very English Virgil at that.

'Mrs. Pidgeon. Like the bird, but with a d. First time ever in a ship. Delighted to meet you, Mr. ...'

'Of course. Forgive me. Mr. Keats, sailing with a Mr. Severn, into the great unknown.'

39

She looks up, puzzled.

'It's Italy we're going to, or so I was told.'

You see, reassuringly literal, after all, and harmless. He surprises himself by taking his place beside her at the table, warms his eyelids in the steam. She neither hurries, nor ruffles him; her slow self-possession makes no demands on him. She is simply there, shaped and a little stooped by the surroundings, as if they'd already taken to her.

'The young lady I've to accompany there,' she continues, 'shan't be joining us till Gravesend. I've only met her the once, I must say, but she struck me as very proper, very charming. No trouble at all, I dare say, and her father was most anxious she'd be in good hands, questioned me closely, wanted to know all sorts of details about me...'

For a moment, Keats fears she's going to tell him everything, then realizes she must be as nervous as himself. He murmurs into the few gaps she leaves and lets his mind wander, taking stock, trying to get some way towards feeling accustomed to the rest of his life. Apart from Mrs. Pidgeon, now recounting her interview, nothing much announces its intentions. A fume of damp, meat and eggs insinuates itself. Six scrawny bunks. A makeshift red curtain hangs askew; ladies to the left, gentlemen to the right. A simple, battered table and four rudimentary chairs. The grimed skylight. A door leading off to the galley, where a clatter of pans

40

suggests the cabin-boy. Otherwise, a muted chamber-piece of groans and creaks. He senses Mrs Pidgeon is looking at him expectantly; has she asked him for his opinion?

'Our new home, then,' he offers.

She studies him for a second, before deciding it doesn't matter that he's not paid heed. She'd hazard life seems rather a trial for him. Out of kindness, she takes him up:

'The strangest home I've ever been in, for certain, Mr. Keats, and I don't mind telling you, by no means my favourite. If I'm not mistaken, I see neither one of us is likely to appreciate it much. I've neither head nor heart for the seas myself. Italy can't come soon enough for me.'

'We'll be seaworthy in no time, I imagine.'

'Oh, we shall last it out, surely,' she grins. 'A few hardships never hurt anyone. Just so long as it doesn't turn out to be our coffin, that's all.'

A lid comes down on his thoughts; he practically flinches. Has she meant to test him? Trap him? What has she heard about him? He feels his mettle sink. All the bad blood wells up in him once again.

'If you'll excuse me, I wonder what's keeping my companion?'

Keeping it down, he fights his way back, brushing irritably at his trousers, back up and out, out, to get a last look of London, breathe its wretched, welcome air,

41

out to where his mourners-in-chief prowl the deck, embarrassed to be of so little use, half way to whistling, waiting for him to reappear.

'Well?'

'Go and see for yourselves.'

How, he wonders, will they make light of that?

Church, early

She'd left *The Half Moon* still sleeping; soon, soon, she told herself as she undid the latch on the side gate, she'd be free of them, dabbed clean of the light film of gratitude she'd been made to feel each day, being kept so publically by her brother and his wife. Down St Peter's alley in her Sunday best, then through the churchyard, scarcely a soul about this early, hurrying as if to a liaison. Ha! No smirking neighbours to nod to, no one worth recognising; only a stilled drunk and a pair of yawning scrawnies wishing day away.

Inside, the tidy Protestant cool and the glimmer of dawn. Perfect, sober sermon-light. Her sure footsteps in the known and quiet. Her sanctuary. Here were all the delineations she needed – dependable angles between the pulpit and her pew; the width of nave and aisles, the marble octagon of the font she always smoothed. Hadn't it been for the best, after all, how she and her Will never did have any children? To have been left alone with them, their always grizzling and wanting mending? The whitewashed walls knew the answers well enough. She could feel the pulpit's eagle watching her come up. God sees everything. Especially all she'd unburdened in his presence: how she'd had to hide what she thought of the sister-in-law; how the laughter she'd shared in had never come near her eyes; how in quiet times, when she hadn't been needed, she hadn't known what to do

43

with herself, had sat on the back doorstep with her head in her hands, wondering how much longer she could stand what she'd become. Her hopeful heart shrank again under His gaze; many a time she'd been made to suspect her own disposition, face how she'd turned out – lukewarm in loving-kindness, holding affection away from her, ever since her husband went. One day, the deep-driven cheer would come back, as if nothing had ever been the matter. She was certain, when once away from her brother, when she had money for herself again, she would find all kinds of willing inside.

This was her chance and she was taking it. Widow's luck; that's what they called it. She'd been quite the sensation. All the feather-ruffling she'd caused, fox in a barnyard. Everyone who knew her had heard her news; *The Half Moon* faithful were in uproar, treating themselves to their opinions, making her listen to their swollen nonsense, their swill. Travelling at her time of life? If all she'd wanted was adventure, there was plenty here what wouldn't mind... Hadn't she heard, they had markets for widows in Naples, couldn't sell 'em quick enough... What she'd endured. They couldn't believe her good fortune, her well-paid way out. Her brother least of all. 'Naples. *Naples*. Look at Lady Hamilton. Didn't do her much good. Riddled with verminous Catholics. Always breeding, always at war. And I bet it's full of Spaniards.' Why put herself through it when she wanted for nothing here? He'd kept this inn all his life, knew

44

all there was to know about travels – other people's, admittedly – got up uncomplaining in the dead of night to let them in, didn't he? All those salt stories and not a single one his own. That was his trouble. To hear him talk, at any one time half of Essex must have been held up at gunpoint, all those vagrants, discharged soldiers and gipsy-beggars on the rampage... 'And you that's never gone further than our sister's out at Marlow.' She'd be mad to go through with it. Her England's to be torn up just like that, then, like a map, with all her husband's things, all her family around her, wishing her well, her in the bosom of it all, and still not satisfied. His red-rimmed, squirrel's eyes helped her decide.

The girl's father had been most particular, somewhat over-protective in the way of one who knows he can't do right by his daughter any more. And she'd sworn in all good faith to be caring and faithful and tender, *just like a mother*, signed a contract which promised nearly as much. How did she know if she had it in her unless she tried? At least the girl had given every appearance of a lovely, lively thing, though a little spoiled, the kind of girl Mrs. Pidgeon wouldn't have minded being herself.

The truth was – and what had brought her here to think through properly – she dreaded the sea, had never gone near it. She had pictures she couldn't help seeing: a dreary, close cabin; the unengaging horizon; grey seas; a sweating, fat captain forever scratching or adjusting himself. Other men, too, strangers at that. And there

45

was bound to be a heavy swell...

Enough of that. Up there was Christ on His cross. To live more like that: unto others. Bowing her head, for the length of several prayers, she had Him all to herself.

'Dear Lord, let me be better than ever before...'

On The Thames

At times, the sun behind cloud, it is molasses, slovenly, crestfallen; at other times, streaked with light, it's sly and indiscreet, a whore's patter, her matter-of-fact undressing.

Most of it looks botched; scrofulous; the slapdash work of an amateur.

Surreptitious so-and-so.

It ought to have more to show for itself, biding, tide-obedient, as if waiting for a dare.

It's noisome, swollen, cursed, as if crossed, as if it couldn't care less, like the century itself.

Everywhere they look, unsuspected slicks of ordure, deadly snags.

A waterman sculls past with his louche, hard-boiled nonchalance, thrashing at the water; a bloated black dog fetches up and is carried off, turning and turning without a yelp, its little legs stiff and ridiculous.

At high-tide, it wobbles its grey jowls from side to side, as if twitching in its spittle-lipped sleep.

Then, pleased with itself for no reason, it hurries on to nowhere in particular.

Further out, it has the sheen of tame pewter, tarnished tankard, a mottled surface much more spit than polish.

In the end, no matter how hard Keats looks, the river has nothing to say to him, its bad stink pervading his grand farewell. Hard to make the necessary gestures, harder still for it to feel heartfelt, with the smell of shit rankling, unmistakable.

Unmoored

Timorously, the *Maria Crowther* works herself free and slides away. None of them – Taylor, Haslam or Woodhouse, Severn having gone to talk with Mrs Pidgeon – can get a word out of him; he stares dumbly at the water's acquiescence, his chin sunk on his chest. The last of the famous monuments gets left behind. He seems to have forgotten his friends are there. If he turned around now, he'd catch them watching him minutely, for signs. It's becoming unbearable, seeing him like this.

Haslam goes over to join him, touches his sleeve, hangs his head in shared sorrow or defeat. For a while, both men stare at the swirls, as if watching from a balcony at the theatre or studying an incident in the street below. A fine-looking girl might well have tripped over, showing her skirts. There's something comical about their earnestness; one of them could nudge the other at any moment, break the river's spell. Disconcerting glimmers of a drowned world swim up. What began as a moment of quiet is uncomfortably prolonged. Only Keats is enjoying this. As if in some obscure children's pact, some wondrous dare, whoever looks up first, will deserve the other man's scorn. Haslam soon gives in; they have to keep trying, can't let him go like this.

'Is it possible, d'you think, to look too long at the one thing?'

Released, Keats breathes in and stretches back,

49

arching his nape up to the skies, eyes closed. No tears at all, though he looks as though he's had his head held under too long. The act of blinking comes across like a rapid warding off, or a warning. And that dry cracked calm is in his voice again, rasping.

'Well, there's not much I'd trust to water.'

That's got them all to come over. Woodhouse and Taylor have that look of wanting to exchange glances but know they can't; Keats is much too sharp for that, well-known for his sizing up, his far-sightedness.

'Other than myself, that is.'

Keats throws them a crafty smile; white crumbs for wading birds. The worry goes out of them like a night's dissipation after a morning's pick-me-up. Woodhouse takes him up:

'Who'd throw themselves in that?'

'Not me! Like drowning in a broth.'

'Still, remarkably busy for a Sunday morning, don't you think?'

'Tides wait for no God, my dear Woodhouse.'

Keats follows them back into the world. Talk returns. Guarded and tense, like an edgy night-watchman hearing the one thing he's been afraid of somewhere out there, where there should be nothing but a thickening silence or a slovenly wind in the trees, he keeps to slivers of prattle, unspectacular observations, the strictly trite. He nods his head when he needs to. When the talk seems in danger of drying up, Haslam thinks of something else.

'Did you hear what Severn said? About his father?'

'Can you believe such a thing?' says Taylor. 'Monstrous in the man. To his own son. As if he feared being overthrown. And for Severn, what a way to begin his Grand Tour. Poor fellow! And he's put so much trust in the antique! How did Severn put it, Woodhouse, about his father's attack?'

'He said he hopes for a kinder reception from the other Old Masters.'

The trick of laughter soon comes back. They make their own entertainment. Scarcely faltering, they latch onto each other's tales, tales that suddenly want to be told, suitably ribald and unwholesome. For a while, Keats seems fine again, voluble, appears to have shrugged off most of his malaise, and when Severn emerges to tell them he's forgotten his passport, their consternation gladly finds an outlet in someone else. Severn takes his stupidity badly, walking up and down, smiting his forehead, feeling every inch the ninny. Never mind it was his father's fault. He won't be reconciled.

'You know, Severn, none of this needed to happen. It's all down to the doctors. Useless, prodding, physicking things. It's all been ordered against my will, against my better judgement.'

It's the first thing Keats has said for some time. And there's more.

'They wouldn't treat a mule as badly as this. Or if they did, you'd hear its bray resound from bank to bank.

51

But we are quieter than that, more dignified. More dignified. And where has this dignity led me to? Here, on a ship of fools, fooling no-one but myself.'

His friends won't stand for that. The protestations fly. Keats is forced to retract, runs a finger down his nose and stares stiffly at his boots. When everybody has calmed down and apologised for one thing and another and plighted their allegiances all over again, Haslam risks a gentle tease:

'At least it's brought the colour to your cheeks.'

'Yes. I said I'm sorry. You know,' Keats says, 'how some fires never go out,' though there's no spark to be seen in him.

A good tidy

'That will have to do.'

The various gentlemen having gone back up, with their variously furrowed brows and their disapproving mouths, and with nothing left to busy herself with, Mrs. Pidgeon is left to reconsider. She's done the best she can. Already, she feels a little less doughty than before. She takes a step back to admire her work, puffing her cheeks, tapping them idly with her fingers. Now she's satisfied, she can listen out. The ship's belly grinds and rumbles, as if something's amiss. She feels like Jonah. That crack she can hear sounds like split wood, sounds just like the crack that goes through the church when the congregation sit back down after singing. No such thing as silence for the next six weeks at least. Even when the boat does its best to be still, it sounds full of the tread of hard-pressed drunks lurching down ancient floorboards searching for the cess-pit.

Cramped she's used to, but there's something wrong here. The cabin wants airing. Its vulgar bareness glares back at her, defiantly. A good tidy has made no difference at all. It still has that poorhouse welcome, that look of the debtors' gaol. Saving what's still in her trunk, she has so few things to brighten it up: a pillowcase embroidered with a rose; her leather-bound prayer-book; her walnut sewing-box; her second-best dress laid out on her bed in the full spread of its austere, dark blue. What else is

53

there to arrange? When she takes her fingers away from her cheeks, the white, chastened marks reach up to her eyes.

No point in fretting. She takes hold of the back of the chair and leans what she's suppressed into it. What had she told herself about moments like this? Sometimes, the only way you ever get on is by simply sitting still. No doubt when she comes on board the girl will liven things up, have some suggestions to make. What's bothering her is how quickly, how visibly, the confidence drained from the young men – those that are coming with her, at any rate. Right from the start, they seemed to be looking to her for too much. The lean pair of them seemed to call out for mothering. What were they looking for? A lonely dowager perhaps! With a shower of loving coins! Oh well! Though she knows full well she shouldn't, she fishes in a pocket for yet another of the barley-sugars which were meant to last her the length of England. She ought to be up with the others making more of the view of London and watching land go by. Nothing to be gained in mouldering down here, being scathing.

'Come on then, girl.'

Pursued by misgivings, she heads for the steps. Wholly out of her experience, all this, as well she might have known. Like she said, she'll feel much better when the young miss comes on board and she can busy herself properly then, getting to like her. She'll have thought of something to cheer herself up with by then. When she

54

gets on deck, she'll acknowledge the men, ask that Mr Keats if he's feeling any better, then leave them to their talk. She'd rather make herself scarce for a bit till she sorts herself out, clamp herself shut. Like oysters do, when seas get rough.

'Which they will.'

Dubious wharves slide by; a wobbly outrageous East Indiaman negotiates past Cuckold's Point, its rows of closed gun-ports towering above them; in Rotherhithe, a quayside squabble animates a low-life couple; Millwall's windmills turn stiffly, out of sequence, prompting Keats to think back to the last time he was this far down the river.

It was only in May. With Brown. Seeing him off. And to think, back then – three, no four months – he'd almost gone with him, for the good of his health! But no, his best friend had left him. Like a guilty runaway, off for adventure's sake and nothing more, Brown had retreated back to darkest Scotland without him. For another, more extensive walking tour. Without him. What good would it have done to have mentioned how distraught that left him? Besides, that had never been his way, to call on another's pity, looking up from his sick-bed with eyes made big and beguiling by illness... He had no energy for ploys, no palate for charity, even though what was at stake was his life.

Keats had gone as far as Gravesend with him. He kept sawing through one emotion after another, making no headway. Everything felt very intense, very decisive. Only the jauntiness of Brown's company sustained his own cheer. At times, Keats was moved enough to pretend absorption in the roared near-misses of the river traffic. No one else – excepting Fanny, in the early days – had ever reduced him to this, having to hide what mattered to him most. With such a friend going, there was bound to be too much he needed to say. By rights, he too should have been high-seasing off to holidays, profiting from the summer, but if he couldn't find it in himself to reprimand Brown, then the fault lay squarely with him, John Keats; he alone had let everyone dear to him go. That's why he wanted to show nothing of what was going on inside. That's why he kept on with the downward stare he had fixed on. For all Brown's breezy good humour, it was important for Keats to appear solemn enough to just suggest his pain. Whatever Keats had been going through, there was no hiding his body was now nothing but a bane. Brown knew *that* well enough. Pretty obvious frailty, when wrapped in a woollen scarf that seemed preposterous in May. Worse, when under May's peerless, generous skies. Out of the wind, Keats felt unseasonably feverish, turkey-stuffed, plumped up and trussed and about to give way to maudlin.

But Brown never noticed things like that; Brown couldn't have cared less; once started, he was never likely to leave off his own story-telling. His commentary on the river-folk continued apace, full of insinuations, spotting yet more types on the banks. One by one, the work-yards opened out, offering up plentiful spawn for his wit: a hump-backed cooper hammering moronically at a barrel, as if driven mad by thirst; a thin, dangling man stood by with what looked like a mouthful of huge iron nails held in his teeth, worn proudly, like a new fashion, or a new kind of penance; a fat-necked woman scrubbed up foam in a bucket, singing full-throated songs of bawdy and loss; all played out against a backdrop of hardship, beggary, theft, with a poor boy running his heart out, both hands cupped out in front of him, dripping with water, or blood.

Where Brown was headed seemed so much simpler, more manageable. Promise had never seemed so pointed and unfair. As the boat threaded its way uncertainly, handling the Thames with a sort of tender diplomacy, Keats felt the gaps between them widen, sundering them, his best friend shearing off at an unapologetically acute angle, like a leather sole ripped from the upper, like a medal stripped from the cloth at a court-martial.

As they rounded another bend, Brown suddenly stopped what he was saying and put his hand on Keats' shoulder.

'The best goodbye, I'm thinking, the *only* goodbye, is a carousing goodbye. Look here, John.'

He produced a bottle from his coat pocket, looking as wily and as proud as the Devil.

'While no one's looking. It's one I've been saving for some time. From the cellar, where else? Let's call it Brown's special reserve.'

Like that, he could conjure new moods and cajole

anyone. So they'd shared one last bottle of claret, alchemical and deliciously dangerous, swigging down pure contraband, against all good sense, all doctors' damned orders. Beloved heady stuff, a last gasp of bad. Nothing, but nothing, better. It was like being schooled all over again in naughtiness, the two of them descending into sly winks and sniggers and why nots. Lips pursed for a long cool draught that brought a better silence, the other eagerly awaiting his turn. The final drops slurped by the river itself.

At the end, Brown waved and waved and waved with all the heart he had. All they'd ever shared and stored was held out in that fluttering flailing gesture, as if repeatedly pivoting wrist and elbow could somehow have conjured love or stayed a terrible loss. As if the desperate to-and-fro of fingers could have said anything more than Brown's squinting, streaming face, turned hopelessly, defiantly, towards the sun's annihilating glare. Soon the man he'd loved more than any other, had grown doll-like, unreadable, his last hurrah grown unintelligible, his form a spidery blur: three years of life together shrunk to a teary blink.

'Look Lethewards, angel.'

Alone upriver, an unseeing Keats had let the loss wash through him, weaken him. He felt glutted and absurd. Beneath him, the river curdled and frothed, wrestling with its contaminations. Willingly, he had gone below, toppled and stunned; all the views had

59

gone. He made another vow: henceforth, adamantine about his heart. Only an ache there, kept to remind him.

Further down

There's a stretch of river, just past Gallion's Reach, where one church tower presides over a vanished parish, where the left bank seems to disappear, giving way to an emptiness, its collapse so complete it draws Keats in, stirring his mood, inviting his disdain. It makes the light open out, making him see more minutely what he's up to, sharpening his need for confirmation into an accusation: how can anyone call that landscape?

He looks out over a mournful scene: pale outbreaks of reeds and bulrushes; beet country; poor man's grazing; drainage ditches, tufted seepage, a half-land succumbed and sodden, weak and freakish, pricked by cries of wading birds. A shrugged-off world, a ragged, fraying sleeve, an occasional land, unsavoury and outcast, whose tentative slopes are at best round-shouldered, whiskery, brow-beaten, prone.

Severn pipes up:

'It doesn't really make for pleasant personification...'

'No.'

Keats intends to cut him short, then relents:

'No, no, how right you are. Not much to write about at all out there. Perhaps a very plain style would do?'

'I don't know about you, but I could barely manage a couplet myself.'

'You, turn to verse? Good God, man. Look at the good it's done me. You stick to your histories. How

61

about we save our respective talents for Rome?'

But now that Severn has mentioned it, maddeningly, Keats finds himself at it once again, like an act of defiance. Before long, a pentameter begins to take shape, starts to whisper to him, like a well-turned apology. Hadn't they warned him about this? Everyone knows the harm poetry can do, dangerously over-loading the mind, weakening it with the compulsion to describe, the bare-faced challenge of the unsayable. *Don't overreach.* Calculus, weights and measures should anchor a swoony mind.

'I bet most people turn away at this point, turn to the other bank, and start looking for Gravesend,' Severn says.

They look at each other.

'The other bank it is,' says Keats

Going to waste

In a low-ceilinged waterfront inn, Miss Cotterell waits for the dark to come down. She has bitten her nails to the quick. Now the index finger of her right hand tingles, sorer than she could have imagined. Her aunt is still with her, for all the use she's been, wretched at her niece's going, at being unable to prevent it. She wears the white face of adult concern, smoothing and pressing her eyebrows, making occasional, tutted observations on the ways of the world, directed mostly through the food going to waste on Miss Cotterell's plate.

'You've not eaten much, have you?'

'You really should try.'

'I can't think there'll be much choice, once you're aboard.'

'Not much in the way of pudding at all.'

Miss Cotterell ventures nothing. Should she reply to any of this? Her aunt doesn't seem to expect it. The steam from her boiled potatoes has come and gone. Sighing, she picks through the bones of her fish. There's a measure of grease on the tines of her fork, tiny flecks of white flesh. It's not just the dread; there's an excitement, too, at work in her stomach. There are two gentlemen due aboard, along with the captain. She folds her napkin in her lap again.

In truth, the last few days alone with her aunt have dragged terribly, waking in a strange house to an assumption of unspoken commiseration. Her aunt fussed about her, in a lather of care, but couldn't keep her own spirits up, let alone Miss Cotterell's, and her compliments – the glow of her niece's skin, the sheen of her hair, her very good teeth – soon seemed too large, like over-generous helpings of the same homemade cake. She's horribly conscious of the trouble she's been; days for her aunt and her cousin of stiff forbearance; long, subdued mealtimes; hushed voices outside her bedroom door, letting her sleep for longer than was good for her; her cousin getting cross over the slightest thing.

That morning at the coach-stop hadn't gone well. She cast about for something to hold onto, an image to fix, but the world was awry. The stubble fields stretched away shorn and useless. The pale pitted road with its careering ruts dropped deep into shadows; the row of inattentive elms and chestnuts just stood there, irritably frisked by the wind. How hard could it be to compress what she felt into a smile? She scratched at something under her sleeve. Her bonnet felt wrong and her dress flapped too loosely against her. Her hands, bonier than ever, hung obvious and unsure of what to hold onto; she should have fetched out her shawl to give them something to do, she should have let them alone, while she continued to stare, looking for the dust trail of the coach and horses.

Her cousin, two years older, was measurably more

composed. She was clearly concentrating. More finished and mature, she kept her sad face on. How, exactly? There was nothing wrong with *her*. *She* wasn't the one being forced away. It wasn't at all fair and it didn't help hiding it and even if it was wrong, she'd go on thinking it. Miss Cotterell pinched her nostrils to fight back tears, snuffled a little. She ought to have gone and sat down and, to keep her spirits up, tried a counting game.

The stage-coach arrived pell-mell, its rickety swagger impressive and vulgar at the same time. The dappling elms leaned away, as if taken aback. Dust dived for cover. The driver reined in at the last moment, showing off. He was badly spattered, but grinning; some harried looks from the Maidstone passengers on high, having endured those roads for miles, attested to the pleasure he took in his work. They clambered down like stiff hurt monkeys, rubbing their knees and buttocks with enthusiasm. Would the blood ever come back? Would the feelings?...

The scrape of a knife on a plate brings her back. A boy is clearing the table. She checks her hair is still in place, senses her eyes aren't still enough, as they stare past her aunt. They widen at the window, as if urging it to reveal something plain enough to remark upon, to take her aunt's mind off things that can't be helped. Barely a passer-by. The odd, inscrutable man. Clouds bedding down for the afternoon, stonily. Restless ships at anchor, chafing against each other. Somewhere amongst them,

65

they'll be putting the finishing touches to the *Maria Crowther*, getting in provisions. Still hours to go. That excitement again. She excuses herself, with that smile. Her aunt practises letting her go without looking round. She is almost out of her hands.

At Gravesend

The river-pilot has gone ashore, his work neatly done. Another trip without mishaps. Soon he will be upriver of them, heading home, his wife expecting him. They watch him being rowed away, between boats, leaning his head back in a long laugh, having forgotten them already.

'What do you suppose goes through his mind?' Severn says, yawning. 'Apart from the river, I mean.'

Keats rubs at his chin, feeling the day's stubble.

'You mean, does he ever think much beyond Gravesend? I doubt it.'

'It must be strange to have each day end in the same place, in the same way, for life to be utterly prescribed.'

'I wonder. Do you think the pleasure in always turning back outweighs the desire to know more?'

'Yes, exactly that! Which are we supposed to prefer? Are we, like him, to live our lives trying to do more with what we have, or are we meant to look beyond our bourn, hanker after more?'

'More what, though?'

It's no good the two of them watching his back more keenly, as if looking for clues, but they do so nonetheless, till he disappears behind a prow.

'Oh well, he's gone.'

'Now we'll never know.'

After a while, Keats goes back to paring his apple.

67

He is learning to keep himself happy. Happy thumbs and useful fingers.

'This one,' he says, 'will be the exact replica of our route down the Thames.'

He pares too slowly, too ambitiously – the fluency has gone from his hand; his knife slips and the paring dribbles to the deck. Look – there goes Greenwich Reach – its far-fetched loop. Keats holds it up, grinning:

'Look, Severn, I give you a sliver of river!'

Since Keats is obviously brighter now, Severn is happy to let him be for a while. Munching his apple, Keats wanders the deck, studies the way the crew get ready. One of them, like a hangman, has to thoroughly check the ropes. They all seem to take the strain. Like these hard-working men, Keats should be keeping his head down, busying himself about something. If only there was something to busy himself with. He can feel his thoughts coming on again. With his back turned, he's free to be as tense as he wants to be, as tight-lipped as a mussel waiting for the incoming tide; his coat gives off the blue-black sheen of the melancholic, the professionally benighted. No matter what he does to gee himself up, all he gets is further in thrall to a clammy unhappiness. He badly needs diverting. Seeing Severn struggling with the news-sheet in the breeze, Keats says at once, still chewing:

'I don't suppose you read about that French woman who followed her husband's coffin all the way to Paris?

68

It took her something like three days. And then, in the cemetery, when no one was looking,' he swallows, 'in a frenzy, she stabbed herself with a pair of scissors.'

Severn puts the paper down, smoothing it on his knee. What, he wonders, is he supposed to make of that? More proof, if proof were needed, of Keats' mischief-making.

'These French. Obdurately passionate, as if sentiment's all they know. Reactions like that help explain Buonaparte.'

'Perhaps she kept them by her for that very purpose?'

'Perhaps.'

'She must have trudged beside him all that time, in all that dust, knowing what she would do.'

'Poor woman.' Severn would much rather talk about something else. His hands fuss with the paper, crimping its fold over and over.

'She must, poor woman, have been beside herself, out of her mind.'

'You overstate the case, surely.'

'Imagine her slogging down the dusty roads mile upon mile, footsore, heartbroken, secretly feeling the sharp steel at her fingertips, feeling its terrible gleam. Its power. What she could do with that power at any time. Loving only that knowledge, that idea of the pain she could put an end to.'

That is an example of the excess Severn must try to keep in check. He will absolutely not be drawn on this:

69

'A wild, womanish gesture. Not worth the scrutiny. I'm surprised at you, Keats.'

Keats senses the admonishment, shrugs and wanders off again, this time to starboard. In the distance, a sense of the estuary, opening up in all its silvered slow, heading far out, immeasurable, always farther out, where all the best secrets are, glinting, untold. Time, for the time being, is very simple, tidal. In actual fact, this is the last low tide he expects dear England to present him. He could always try to surmise a bit more time away, give way to September's drift, suppose another world to no real purpose, imagining himself gaudily, breezily, out there with the pleasure boats, or idly man-o'-warring, now that France has been defeated...

Beneath him, imperceptibly, the servile, addict Thames slithers out, leaving upturned, shame faced slime banks furrowed with rivulets, ruffed and spotted with creamy, yellow froths, like a leprosy-necklace against a harlot's décolletage. Somewhere safe and sorrowing on the other side must stand Fanny, pearled and freckled, wrinkling her nose against the weak sun. He hopes she's not thinking overmuch of him. Here, for company, he has the trickling dregs of Gravesend, mottled and bristling with river-weed, rank and sooty-buttery.

The afternoon has gained on them obtusely; Severn was meant to be keeping an eye on it. The sky is yet more overcast, threatening. The quarter-hours must

70

have sounded and gone, without his realising. A ruckus of clanging bells advertises evensong. Keats feels partly cheated, partly relieved. So caught up have they been in the weighty complex trick that every self-respecting Englishman observes – namely, hiding what he feels – they've forgotten to mark the sad slide into dusk. Dark clouds have ushered it in early. When the drizzle sets in, the climate's mean farewell, they duly repair below, but that little moment of lingering, with the sudden wet on their hair and surprised faces, is surely the last they'll see of daylight England. When Keats' right palm lets go of the handrail, followed by the inadvertent half-look over his shoulder at the looming grey, the far shore has already gone. Once in the cabin, they find the portholes have misted over.

Severn was disappointed with the twilight. In no uncertain terms. Passing itself off in murk like that, virtually unremarked. No call for wiliness of that sort. With its passing, all the putative calm of late evening at the river's edge, all Keats' hopes of a lingering lovely leave-taking – all the curve and charm of sunset – gone too.

Since then, they've been peering through the portholes at unrelieved drizzle, trying to hear it, and thinking about women – mothers, sisters, lovers. Scarcely distinguishable lamps sway up and down river. Impossible to trust them, gauge the right distance. Somewhere out there, the tide must be scampering in. His friends have been gone close to two hours and neither Keats nor Severn has said a word on the subject. They are reading, off and on. They feel tied to each other, hemmed in.

Mrs Pidgeon's charge has still not arrived. Don't say she's been let go? Or should that be reprieved? She can't decide which would be worse. The gentlemen are terribly subdued. She honestly doesn't know what to think. She thinks about the money. About what she's been given to understand, the assurances she's been given. She couldn't be more nervous before an audience with the king.

About eight o'clock, a rowboat nears, choppily slicing the dark. That must be her. They must go up at once, brave the drizzle and damp. Mrs. Pidgeon plucks at her neckline for the umpteenth time.

Here she comes now, the long-awaited, perilously fashionable and frighteningly, eagerly eighteen, wrapped against all misadventure, as if she'd just stepped out of Vauxhall Gardens, something faint and orchestral still playing in her ears, still flushed from men's attentions, moving in an air fraught with suggestion, with the promise of further endearments. Who would be next to murmur sweet assignations? There are practised eyes out there, taking their exercise. Father said as much. Devils in summer sleeves crunch the gravel walks, hands behind their backs. How men bide. Beware the sudden whispered imputation; see the knowingness of those looks, where they're leading – all the attendant lost virtues, their white trains spoiled in the dust.

It must seem like a dream to her: here are the rough, muffled voices, half-recognised; the flimsy, squirming rope-ladder flung over the side; the solemn slap of the waves; the unsteadiness about her heart; the strong grasp of a strange man's hand; the perfect night for an elopement.

She hurries too much to be considered dainty, but the puffy squint of the moon trying to peer through seems to suits her, little waif-wraith. Her pale dress floats about her nicely. The two men step aside; once she's thanked the captain and looked around the deck, gathering herself, Severn nimbly manages

73

the introductions. Performs them, rather. Despite some tiresome simpering, the girl has an engaging freshness, borne on the high tide of her curiosity. She's been delayed at her aunt's insistence, it seems, but the evening has turned out mild and well-meaning after all. And when she laughs, suddenly, lightly, for no reason, the hoarseness in it comes at Keats like an outrage, an unjust provocation, almost a physical blow; he recognises the signs immediately. She, too, is dying, dying of consumption. Not, after all, sailing to meet her brother, but trying, like Keats, for an impossible cure. Oh, she is unfailingly pretty and doomed and will for weeks on end be intimate with him, and hear him cry out what could be anything in his sleep.

Keats tucks himself into a shadow as soon as he can; holds on to some wet rigging. He screws his eyes shut. All of this is of course happening for a reason. Now more than ever he feels the ironies swarming again. So, his prick-tease, sardonic fate will be with him all the way, best guardian. Sweat breaks out on him; his nerves flare up, like phosphorus. Severn, meanwhile, is delighted and has no intention of hiding it. His conversation pulses with *by all means* and *naturallys*. He practically swims towards her. You could almost read by the light of his willingness to please. What confidence in his blond curls!

Once she's been shepherded down the steps by the captain and Mrs. Pidgeon, Severn goes straight to Keats' side, hissing his effusions.

74

'Keats, Keats, tell me I'm right. A very attractive young lady. Wasn't Aphrodite born out of the waves?'

Keats knows it's only right to play along. 'Ah but she was Greek and what's more, naked, and didn't emerge, as far as I recall, gasping for breath, hauled up by the hairy hand of a certain Captain Walsh.'

'Didn't I tell you I'd been studying the classics? I swear, those are the looks I've been seeing!'

'I thought you could only afford cheap prints and engravings? Don't tell me – now you've seen the real thing, you're going to have to have a closer look? A private viewing?'

'Close study is essential to the true artist. But, at the very least, she'd make a worthwhile muse for an otherwise uneventful voyage, you'd agree?'

'Uneventful? Not if you can help it, by the look of you. Either way, her acquaintance shall be all yours, whether you will or no. But mark my words. There's nowhere to sulk on deck if you make a fool of yourself, and show your hand too early; there'll be no long walks with Keats on the heath to revive your hurt sparrow-feelings. Sobbing for love in the galley with the galley-boy won't do.'

'I don't mean to win her, Keats!... Just to marvel...'

'Marvel away. Let's go down and you can begin your studies in earnest.'

Below, the ladies seem on the verge of a commotion. Mrs Pidgeon seems less than enchanted; the girl has

75

grown so much thinner. When Miss Cotterell finally gathers herself and turns to see them, with their forced smiles and china cups held out like charms against the swallowing dark, the pretence goes out of her like grain from a split warehouse sack. Oh the intimacy, the dinginess of the scene. Impossible – these men – not at all what she'd – and in such... Weirdly elongated in the wobbly candlelight, their faces lean into her, nodding and wishing her all manner of well. Under their scrutiny, she senses her knees beginning to buckle. She is close to calamity. What was meant to be no more than a sigh comes out wailing and remote. Mrs Pidgeon fishes for her little bottle of remedies.

'Look sharp, gentlemen, the lady's in distress.'

They dutifully fumble for her, gasping like unmannerly porters catching at baggage thrown from the coach's roof. Yet Miss Cotterell regains herself at once, gripping the table-top, and manages a grey, watery smile of her own; she stammers her excuses. Keats helps her into a chair, eyebrows raised, eyes wide with knowing, explaining as much as he can to Severn in one look. *Seen enough? This girl is ill, I know it; I recognise myself in her; all her symptoms are mine.* They all know better than to say anything until Miss Cotterell does:

'Thank you, thank you, I'll be fine in just a minute.'

Little by little, conventions come back, like well-fed guests patting easily their stomachs, expecting cigars. Mrs. Pidgeon sweeps into action – she has a

76

way with compassion – hushing up any lingering show of emotion, her fingers pressing composure into Miss Cotterell's upper arm.

'There, there,' she tenders. 'It's all come as a shock now, hasn't it? We'll soon have you right.'

Severn nudges a cup of tea towards the two women.

'Well, there's nothing like an entrance!' he remarks. 'We never normally have that effect, do we, Keats?'

Her smile is more rounded now, more grateful than apologetic.

'I fancy, sir, I'd rather like to join you, if I may, at your tea. I regret to say I've not been well this summer, not at all myself. That's why I'm here, heading south, for somewhere better, better, at any rate, for me.'

She doesn't have to say any more. For a moment, Mrs Pidgeon looks horrified, takes her hand off the girl's back, as if she'd been caressing a wasp, managing only to disguise her shock as they shift to take their places.

'The south will be better for us all,' murmurs Keats. Now that she can look about her and take her measure of them, they can see, for all her regret, the girl is reassuringly rosy-cheeked, and with the reddish-gold shine of her curls reaching down obediently to her shoulders, she looks the robust epitome of English. Something about her – willingness, gratitude, propriety worn lightly – would make a gentleman inclined to bring out often her colour and smile. In some less scrupulous, Keats imagines, there'd be no end of trying.

77

Keats can already see Severn framing a genial question. It's true that an unfortunate lapse rarely looked so prettily bewildered, as the girl stares strangely about her. To beguile away the hours for her would make a merry pastime. Or would have once. For now, a deal of appropriate small talk seems called for.

They go through the introductions once more, as best they can, but the girl remains troubled, her replies uncertain. There's too much to take in. Her head is swimming. What could be more eloquent of their terrible circumstance than these three nodding, smiling strangers? They approach her as if they'd landed the extraordinary, as if she spoke, in whispers, another language, as if she were some discovery of theirs, something unparalleled, straight out of a fable.

What she hears from them is unbearably familiar. Why does everyone she's met since she first took ill seem to have rehearsed the same tired lines? No wonder she sickens! Is there some book of trite condolences every one of us must learn by heart? All their studied words – heartfelt or otherwise – ring hollowly through her head. Try as they might, she can taste the false cheer and won't partake. She lets them say what suits them.

'Of course we'll all see summer again.'

'Italy will be full of marvels, full of a soft healing warmth.'

'Good grief, child, you'll be fine. We're all of us here to help.'

78

To reassure her, Keats lets on he's had years of medical training, at Guy's, in London, with some of the greatest surgeons of the day. What he omits to mention is in the detail; the blood-letting and the useless frantic stanching, the sweat starting on foreheads, the committed rasp of the handsaw, the smell of shit and piss, the calling out for God and mother.

'But one thing I can promise you. There'll be no more privations, no starvation diets. We have left all that behind. We can even start to enjoy ourselves. Besides, there's every chance of a smooth passage, even in September.'

Miss Cotterell sips her tea, holding her cup in both hands, steadily now. When she tries to look up and beyond it, the two men appear slightly out of focus, looming awkwardly like waiters, two hazy stand-ins for her father, a pair of unlikely protectors. Mrs. Pidgeon, ready to move on, begins to regale her with the story of her day, and when Severn tells them about the Captain's search for a goat – 'of all things' – in Gravesend, they finally settle into the matter-of-fact.

Keats can't resist: 'You think that unlikely? Well, let's just say – I hope you're ready for this – I kid you not.'

Of the two kinds of star

The black river churns unguessably. A little moonlight has stayed out, unedifyingly. Too many boats block any view. But the stars? That's what he's come out to gauge, having waited for the breaks in the clouds. There are several up there tonight, some of them familiar. Maybe they can explain these feelings. What, if anything, do they connive at? Do they even notice him, looking up?

Do they, as he's beginning to think, truly map our lives? Could they really be the souls he'd like to think they are, various and chosen? If so, there's plenty to look up to and admire: there's certain boldness up there, gleaming with pride, perhaps, at what they achieved in their time. Gloating, now, mocking him. They seem to flicker with criticisms. He feels their judgement-light condemn his failing spirits.

But whilst some beat strongly, others weaken. What do those ones mean? Do they mean harm? Which amongst them is the fateful star, the one marked out for him, the baleful one, the ironic one, stalking him through the night?

PART THREE

The Channel

Late September 1820

Middle bunk

Miss Cotterell lies awake, prickling with self-consciousness, as still as she can make herself. Only her eyes dare rove, unhappily. She forbids the rest of herself to move. If she's quiet enough, she hopes, and slows her breathing sufficiently, she might eventually convince herself she's not really there. She is not despairing, no, though turned on her side, she makes a mournful seashell shape, humped around a little hollow.

There's not much room for gestures, anyway. The slats, which are to keep them from sliding out when the sea roughs up, prevent an extravagant stretch. She lies there, stuck with her resolve, listening in to the ship's relentless hurdy-gurdy of groans, willing them to work

81

their lulling. Nothing goes on happening for a long time. In the end, she reaches up and allows herself a few plaintive strokes on the rough planks of the bunk above her – the rough of a lover's stubble, perhaps? – where Mrs. Pidgeon is sound asleep. Then she feels for the paleness of her cheeks, smooths at the roundedness of lips that make no sound and gives her fingers a timorous kiss. There now.

The gentlemen opposite, murmuring bits of conversation from behind the curtain, must be wondering what on earth she's introduced them to. Of late, wherever she goes, as soon as she coughs, she brings the most unwanted consequences. People she knows well keep a measurable distance, beyond respectful. Eyes narrow dreadfully. Excuses are rapidly made. Society! She might as well have had some deformity. Which would at least account for their distress. She might as well have said what she was really thinking, speak the truth. See them run at that!... Of course, on the voyage, they will all be together, in close quarters, come what may...

In which case, whom might she prefer – the painter or the poet? Goodness knows, if her father was with her, he'd soon know what to make of them. She supposes, if she were forced to pick, that her choice would light on Mr. Severn: he looks decidedly the better bet. Taller and with a sprightly, solicitous air; her father would grudgingly approve. Mr. Keats, for all the intensity in

82

his brows, makes her feel uncomfortable, seems to know too much of what she may be forced to go through. Besides, he's short and gives the impression of keeping things from others. She could do worse than give Mr. Severn the benefit of her glances, but would he show any sign of having noticed; in roughly four weeks would she have time to oversee a worthwhile dalliance with him? What were the lines from that song again, that one at Drury Lane? Something about ruin. Oh, how did it go? How did any of it go? But yes, the more she thinks about it, it would be him she favoured; she likes the feel of his future, the dash about him, heading for nothing less than Rome. Now she has no chance of easily getting off to sleep. Nothing she can do but stare some more, pick through the end of an awful summer, think back to the life she knew...

Most days, she'd been consigned to a sedate walk to the bottom of the garden where the day-lilies bloomed, to while away the afternoon sheltered there in the sun-trap by the high brick wall. That was as close to pleasure as she could get, sat there with her eyes closed, in last year's bonnet and shawl, amongst the bees, glad of their company. Grateful not to be thinking, for a change, of her lack of progress, her no improvement.

Father had made everything worse when he'd said he wouldn't be able to spend as much time with her as he'd wanted. This was the end of June when fewer friends were coming to call – her illness deemed

83

no longer interesting by then. Apparently, he had become more and more important to the office – she couldn't imagine the paperwork required for all those shipments. What was certain, was how more and more often he'd been away on business which required all of his – and only his – experience. Why did fathers get like that? 'Some men retreat from the least complication,' said her aunt, who seemed to know. He had been like that once before, when she had objected to his choice of governess. Now, when it most mattered, he had proved distant and irritable, sat deep and stunned in self-made glooms at the dinner table, his whiskery face skewered by shadows, his mood a nurtured bruise. He still wrote letters to her, when he was called away, but in his rather more ragged, late-evening hand, urging her to follow his advice, believe in his excuses.

By August, hardly anyone dropped by; her friends had been invited out to the country estates; she imagined them skittish and pent-up and bobbing foolishly for men in spacious rooms designed to make them feel overawed and humble. She thought of them a great deal, out there in the world, withholding themselves carefully, as the value of their virginities soared.

At home, the new maid-of-all-work was shier than ever; curtseying defensively, answering in a rush of monosyllables, dropping one or two things. Sunday services over at St. James that she used to so look forward to had had to come to an end. Father had decided that

84

too. Some sermons he considered a little too spirited; and there was always the danger of too much exposure – all that murmuring from the pews at the back when she came in, all that rolling or averting of wealthier ladies' eyes. Instead, she learned defiance in her private prayers, which grew more demanding of God as the summer wore on.

Each week, her aunt sent her a new novel, but it soon stopped mattering which; the outlandish plots with their simpering characters swirled around her, utterly unbelievable; too many fine manners, too many fine longings, an imprecision of indecisions; so much revolved around what didn't happen in an English garden; everyone overheard what was meant to be secret. And she couldn't have cared less about the endings.

Why was there so much advice in the world, anyway? It was all intended for her and her good and it all came so pointed and often and free. August just got hotter and hotter; she wasted whole afternoons at her toilet, dabbing at herself like a sore. She tried out yet more perfumes, pulling a face each time. Flasks and miniature bottles crowded her dressing table; she would fiddle with tinctures, prise open her jewellery box and contemplate trying another ill-fitting necklace that would slope down past her throat like a smear of expensive tears. As if there were some remedy hidden somewhere for being like this, she rifled through the cabinet drawers, knowing full well no amount of knacks

85

would help. All along her secret heart was telling her to abscond, abscond, a palpable drum-dare beating on – why listen to what doctors said, what neighbours recommended, what well-wishers wished on her? She should have just dashed out as she was, out under some headlong, hopeless shower, England's maddening rain finishing her off in an unrepentant drench, her long skirt thrilling in the soaking grasses, as she blinked back the downpour, wet seeds clinging to her hemlines and her hair... But did she ever? What *was* that lack in her?

It was more or less the same with the vicar. She'd kept him loyally coming by and showing his interest long after it was clear she no longer wanted it. When he'd dropped by again, at the beginning of September, and the two of them had been left alone, she had finally decided to put an end to his attentions. No more porcelain manners, no more wan upbraiding from his gently chiding voice; no more heavy-liddedness as he described his ideal parish.

Her father had teased her about him from the start, saying he'd never be persuaded out of his text. The apocryphal daughter. For three months, it had excited her, noting the increasing frequency of his visits. Then the illness came. That winter she just got weaker and weaker. Still he kept his visits up, throughout the spring and summer. Was it love in him? Or was it force of habit? He was the kind of man who gradually came to a standstill in his intentions and stayed there. Now, since

86

nothing much mattered anymore, given she'd been told to go abroad, she could afford to be unfair at last, could refuse to fill in the silences, refuse to tailor herself to him. He was, in any case, too easily anticipated. That earnestness of his, that she once half-forsook, half-forgot herself over, now seemed more like dreariness, and dogged dreariness at that.

Apparently, the list of things for her to be afraid of was on the increase: draughts were especially devious in late summer, as were modish gentlemen, inklings of inexplicable passion, several kinds of vanity and, above all, Rome. She was almost caught out by his perceptiveness, till she realized he was simply rehearsing for his sermon later on that week. When she sighed and folded her hands in her lap, he looked up in genuine surprise; what he'd planned to say trailed off amid dark furniture. Reaching into his pocket, he held out, almost triumphantly, a slim, black volume to her. Of commentaries, no less.

'There are a number of passages I have marked out especially.'

She didn't move. He waited for her, something he had always done so well, expecting her to reach out and take the book; she made him wait long enough to realize she had intended to slight him. He coloured then, and when she finally took it from him, she put it face down beside her and folded her hands back again. How very childish it all seemed now. That hairline crack of a smile

87

had appeared on his face again. She had looked at his glum, sweating palms, and felt nothing.

'It has been a very difficult time. I very much regret to hear of your going. That we shan't be seeing you at our services for some time fills me...'

At the window, the black beech stirred and flared in the stiff, September breeze, dominating the garden. It was still a grasping, magnificent thing full of rustling dark flames. How many times had she sheltered there, under its sibilance, found peace beneath its glimmering reds and bronzes? Now it cast its purple shadow over her whole ruined summer. She took up her station by the tall windows to see properly how it obscured almost everything. Meanwhile, the vicar, watching her rise and walk away, pressed on, desperately changing tack.

'You have decided on Italy, if I am not mistaken?'

She turned and nodded at this, the slenderest of encouragements.

'Well, what I'd like to say is that we think highly of you here in the parish, Miss Cotterell, very highly, as I say. And as you know, I have been very much indebted to you – and to your father of course. You have both been very attentive to me from the moment I arrived really, and you must know your leaving will be a great loss to me, a great personal loss. You should know I shall of course be keeping you very much in my prayers and in my thoughts, until your joyful return next summer, when I should like to be, if not the first, then one of the

88

very first, to congratulate you on your recovery...'

She cared not to answer. She did not care for his confessional manner, either. Presumptuous now that it was too late, and vacillating when she had given him the opportunity, he had been a singular disappointment. A cold grate is no place for an ember. Oh well. At least she had never given herself away. Her best friend, she knew, would have chosen this moment to make him leave in silence, his thick fingers revolving the rim of his hat, her face all the while buried in her hands. She at least had the courage to look at what she did to the man. To have felt his unspoken love hang over her head, like an absolution, would have been unbearable; she couldn't have countenanced the thought of him standing there, forever failing to know where to look. The defeated, black-haired backs of his hands. Coolly, unsatisfactorily, she'd heard herself say:

'Please, there's no need...'

And though he'd managed to keep talking till the tea-things were brought in and was somehow able to finish the huge slice of fruit-cake she offered him, with as little as that, she'd dismissed him. She had seen him into his summer coat, watching him turn up his collar and step out resolutely into the shower of rain. He wouldn't meet her eyes. She waved him off, though he didn't turn round, simply made his way home through an unsuitable, ungainly country, its promises dashed by storms, its flower heads damaged and broken. And that had been that, after all. Back inside, she'd leant against the door and stared at her shoes on the polished floor, their delicate black bows.

She'd had no wish to go back to the drawing-room, no desire to sip at the stewed tea or examine the swarthy oils of hunting scenes, fields full of contented livestock, straggling copses – her father's eighteenth- century taste – that had stared down for so long at the two of them, no desire at all. By the piano, her favourite sheet-music had long since been tidied away. Her Haydn. His sweet-solemn airs. All around her, settling into a comfortable late-afternoon gloom, were the rooms she'd grown up in, rooms in which she'd listened to stories, had her astonishing tantrums, childhood fevers; had earned a heapful of her father's affection and praise, richly-deserved since she studied so hard; rooms where she'd taken the measure of her girlish self, made the discoveries that matter, the quiet leaps and breakthroughs, where she'd got away with countless self-indulgences. And the room where mother had died.

Storm coming, off Brighton

Seen across such an expanse, a frigid level, without a distraction in sight, the storm-burst stalks the length of the horizon. They are drawn to stare at it, as if under an obligation, their faces draining, haggard with alarm. This is how quarry must feel. The air has changed, smells sulphurous, full of salt-menace. To the four of them, unused to anything like this, it looks like an annihilation. They've no chance of outrunning it. Already they seem to be teetering, as if on the blade-edge of the world, delivered up to the mercy of something obviously merciless. A terrible hush precedes it, like the hush that passes through the crowd at Tyburn; the whole sky sets and stiffens, its features stricken, in a paralysis. Then the wind rips in.

'We'll never shake this one off, Severn,' shouts Keats, into the gale.

'You don't say.'

'Did you expect any less?'

'With your luck?' The wind contorts Severn's grin into a grimace. As if he's laughing in the face of danger.

Clenching and darkening, it approaches, like a pang of jealousy that burgeons and blackens all it cares to look on. In the distance, it teems to no avail, dark tentacles of rain hanging loosely down, as if dragged against their will. How the whole mass churns and flexes, wrestles with the burden of itself.

91

What a waste of rain, Keats thinks, as he sees it sweep in and pummel the unsteady, sickening ocean; drowning in its own element, it pocks the surface in exasperation, its energies dissipated far from any shore where it could do some good, dying long before it should. Anywhere else, say The Downs or Lowland Belgium, rain like this would ripen and refresh, force up autumn blooms. Here, it falls for no reason.

The storm so completely matches and outdoes his mood, Keats can't hide the admiration in his voice. The most extreme case of contrariness for contrariness' sake he's ever seen. The thrill of it leaves him breathless, happily stating the obvious:

'It looks like Drury Lane out there. We'll be having the full spectacle tonight.'

'I've seen enough already. You'd better come too.'

'I'll be down in a minute.'

Severn looks at him. 'Make sure you are.'

Keats only lets go of the rail, when the first big drops start to spatter, retreating from what appears to have swollen into a judgement, a great and timely warning.

When he gets below, he's amused to find he holds a tightly-wound handkerchief, twisted round and round his ring finger.

'At least it's letting us know we're alive,' he announces, wild and barely recognisable. Nobody hears him. In any case, they're all concentrating on their stomachs' vaulting acts.

92

And when it finally hits the ship, all four of them supine in their bunks, faces lit by dread or revelation, all of them looking up as if expecting the Almighty, it pounds and harries and lashes at them, demented, frantic, tearing like a wolf's claws at the casement, scrabbling to be let in.

They have built their house of sticks.

Severn sees for himself

He'll never speak ill of mountains again. There's real steadfastness for you. Despite a winter's worth of inclement weather, low cloud's frequent shifting attentions, fogs of low intent, their veiled bulk never moves, massed on the horizon, their fortitude exemplary. As dependable as the dawns and dusks they let through.

The cold green towers and teeters above him, drawing itself yet monstrously higher, its whale-lungs filling and filling, like a bellows that beggars belief, like a colossal slingshot pulled tauter and tauter, unnaturally distended, protracted, firing itself into foam and wrath and plenty, dwarfing him, Joseph Severn, the miniaturist, squirming there, head-to-toe trepid, pissy and tiny, holding for all his worth onto nothing more than a rope. A rope! When what he needs is chains of iron! He feels like the pip that first squeaked; he croaks like a frog in a grip.

As he scutters across the deck, blinking like a seven-year-old at the enormity, he readily admits the image that's been pounding away at him the moment he slammed the cabin doors behind him – his father. Father, scandalized and betrayed, puffed up and impossible to predict, wholly enraged and deranged, coming for him, crippling him with fear. That's what he's come to contend with. The old man's roars appal his head:

94

'Take that and that and that, you shit!'

But he withstands.

Later, there's another voice drowning his hammering heart out. It's coming from him all right, in fits of screeches – 'Mistake! Mistake!' – but he can't hear a thing, crouched in his disbelief. Looking up at the sea – can this be possible? The surface of the earth – and with it, the sense it made – free-falls away from him. The cradle and all its blankets whipped out from under him. Wishing he could see stars. Weak-kneed and spellbound, he tries to ride the diagonals, but he feels himself at the tipping-point, swung out from normality, repeatedly calling on God. All's in the lurch, shifting, awash. Otherworldly. He can't get a fix on his position. He scrabbles like a rat along the slabbering deck, slippery as turds. How on earth does he get his purchase back? 'Bail out, bail out!' Now, while there's still some honour, some thought gone into his cowardice, before the funk ripples through him and he can't move, abandoned to his fate.

Captain Walsh looks over at him in horror. As if he'd just discovered a species of endangered gentleman, a half-emerged highly-civilized life-form farcically out of its element.

'Someone get a line around him quick!'

Before anyone can rescue him, what gets Severn seeing sense is a cataract's worth of spray emptied out on him. It hits him like a rite of passage: dousing the

95

buffoon. The slithering idiot. A thoughtless clown having to think for dear life, then think again. The fear goes right through him, parching his throat. What he realizes is that what seems like power is actually helplessness. What he's witnessing are the sights and sounds of torment, persecution. The English Channel in agony. How it wails and writhes, doing battle with itself, dashed and dashing, thrashing without reason, fomenting nothing, poor, bemused thing unable to help itself. Brother-waves are set against each other, pulled and pummelled this way and that, by a grievous wind. This ceaseless lurching is the sea's predicament, its resurgent cry for help. Truly, the waves are simply sent reeling from each other, glassy-eyed and greying-green, glazed over, as if punch-drunk.

There is, he should have known, a pattern in this, a grander scheme at work. To find yourself in the trough, at the nadir, there's always a second's worth of wallow to endure before the slow inextricable climb – like the filling of a syringe – up the enormous wave-wall. Though Severn's convinced he's seen enough to make it back to the safety of the cabin, there's nothing for it but to skivvy on his hands and knees, sud-soaked, like the scouring-girl, her master standing over her, criticising and desiring her, pointing out the bits she's missed.

'Remind me,' says Severn later, rough-towelling and shaking his bedraggled, leaky, tomfool head, 'never to go up there again in weather like that. I swear to you, prevent me, at whatever cost to your dignity. Implore my religion. Oppose me outright. Speak ill of my mother. Impale me with my brushes. Shiver, if you so wish, my timbers. Don't, whatever you do, hesitate to separate a fool from his folly. If you see that look in my eyes – that all-whimsical, all-visionary roll – then snap it out of me. Bind me to the nearest mast.'

'Like Odysseus?' laughs Keats.

'Like who?' Severn stops roughing up his hair. 'Yes, Odysseus, why not? Like Odysseus. For example.'

Putting about

Ominous for hours, like the rumble of the plague-cart backwards and forwards outside a marked door, then buffeting, manic. They hold on frantically to what they can believe in. Their possessions slide about, hissing and banging, like spirits demanding to be let out. Light reels from the storm-lantern slicing through the dark, splashing fear on their zoo-faces. The four of them, peering from their burrows, try to gauge each other's helplessness, the curtain having long since slipped to the floor. No decency, no privacy in a storm. Like cowering children lost in a misadventure, their eyes pop and dart around them – but the storm comes on from every direction. They expect a sundering at any moment, dread calls from above, the ship's sides wrenched apart. At any moment.

A crack no louder than the others, and the immodest sea is amongst them, swamping without discernment. The walls, the towers of England have been breached. Barbaric, its smeared beard trailing foam, it gluts in seconds. A little spume conveys its relish; the maw is smacking its lips, gregarious in its savagery.

A brief, thrilling pause, and then they can't hear anything but the boom and wrath. Keats, oddly, dangerously elated, sees poor Miss Cotterell's mouth stretched open. Nothing comes: her lungs aren't strong enough to fill for a scream. Her eyes have forgotten to blink; bulbous and strained, as huge as a horse's eyes at the gallop, they alone render her terror.

Then, the way an animal that's been hunted down for miles, hiding in its muddy brake, its big heart hammering, makes one last bid for freedom, Mrs Pidgeon shins back up to her bunk at the top, in a whirl of heavy skirts and underskirts. She cuts a surprising dash. And the words she comes out with, the English! Every syllable distinct between the buffets. All pretence has gone. On her hands and knees, imperilled as never before, she kicks at the rumpled sheets that snag her legs and worries at the mattress, as if looking for the mask she's lost. Finally, she sinks down, covers her face with her hands. As if a mummer played Death. That's the last they'll see of her till it's over. There isn't any more.

The most appalling minutes go by. Severn counts them all, because that's all he can think of to do. Only after a long lull does he finally break off from his numbers and look down with genuine anguish, wincing at his trunks' colliding – all his papers, his sketches, his letters of introduction are in there! He fears for his future commissions. He sees his tours of the best palazzos cancelled at short notice. Worse, he thinks he can see, any second now, his favourite colours running and spoiling, seeping out in a pallid rainbow, forlorn rose, mauve and violet bruising into brown, there where the rainbow ends.

99

Meanwhile, from his vantage-point, gleeful Keats is about to cheat what death had eyed up long ago. All his suffering and his knowledge of the suffering to come could be sluiced from him in a moment; he attains an absolute clarity. Won't its cold please cover him over and swirl him down, down, in thrumming spirals, tumbling him, completing him, filling his lungs to the brim with ever colder cold? He's the only one who hasn't been religiously crossing himself. This is it! This is it! This is Death coming on, clamorous, preposterous, out of nowhere, out of the immense, amorphous grey-green-blue!

Last shore leave, Lulworth

The two crew chosen to row them ashore could scarcely be more loathsome. They have an air about them of regularly apprizing the gaudiest of women at a bawdy-house. Those soiling looks they exchange should not have to be borne. Must she sit fast as they shamelessly glower and leer at her? She won't engage with their kind. All her costly schooling is trained on the horizon. She feels the indignity coiling and cooling around her heart. So, she is to be spared nothing, forced to grow up in company like this. 'Shield your eyes in that case,' her father would have said. Try as she might, she keeps losing that tune she carries in her head for occasions like this. She really ought to have complained of a headache and left the gentlemen to it. No doubt men of refinement like to stride up and down the coast, exerting and asserting themselves, stopping their talk from time to time to consider the state of the tides. Whereas for poor Miss Cotterell, prolonged, intimate conversation with Mrs Pidgeon – the kind a young woman lives for – already seems unwelcome; ever since the storm, she's noted something scornful and impatient about her companion, grown clucking and sour, like an egg gone bad, though quite what Miss Cotterell has said to offend her... Yet another mystery. How many more lessons will there be? Still, it's probably her last chance of England. The two of them can surely walk about a bit.

101

Land will do them all some good. Besides, she must be less extravagant in her self-denial, bearing in mind the Atlantic, and whatever else is to come.

The cove itself has much to commend it, its fan-shape elegant and inviting. In full September sun, its white cliffs rise sheer and brilliant, dazzling the small waves which break harmlessly over shingle. At the prow, Mr Keats and Mr Severn are murmuring like school friends and though she can pick out one or two words – 'Fingal's Cave; overwhelming pressure; nothing like it since' - they remain bent in some secret business: mischief or melancholy, impossible to gauge.

By the time she has been helped ashore, most attentively by the gentlemen, she feels a little better. She watches the two of them saunter away, entirely in cahoots. Fortunate to have such close friends, she supposes. With her blessing, Mrs Pidgeon sets off in no ascertainable hurry at all to inquire after refreshments, leaving her some time to be herself. From a good dry rock she's pleased she found by herself, she squints up at the thoroughly provoking sun, wrinkling her nose, shuffling pebbles between her hands. Her freckles will come out, if she's not careful.

She wonders where her father could be now. It would be nice to think she occupied him in some way, as he steps out from the office, into the thick of Borough, perhaps stopping off at the baker's for a treat for later. Apple turnover's her favourite. Nothing for her anymore, of course. And there she goes again. This is the very trouble she's been having with herself. This is what comes of finding herself all alone in a queer, empty cove, where the fishermen must have struck out before dawn, leaving a straggle of dowdy, downtrodden cottages smoking mournfully till their return. And the place is so quiet: a few gulls, and the waves modestly breaking, in a hush, as if sensing the presence of a lady. And the road climbs so steeply, quite beyond her, scrawling its way into unimaginable England, lost behind hills, rolling away as green and elusive as ever...

Well, she is having none of it, as she fidgets with her shoe, sliding a finger under the stocking where a stone is hurting. Beauty's where you want to find it. There must be more than this to this shut off corner, this forgotten hunch of England's cold shoulder with its misshapen rocks and its deal of wilderness. Besides, is it any worse, having fetched up bored and alone here, than if her aunt, having insisted on her coming round by four, were to leave her to wait in the back parlour, the table neatly set, the ornamental clock regularly upbraiding her lack of self-sufficiency? Well, is it?

Then, about a hundred yards away, that girl she'd scarcely taken notice of before stands up and appears to look in her direction. With no other gesture, no word at all, she has got Miss Cotterell's attention. It just needed a supplicant's look, one that Miss Cotterell knows so well, whenever the door to her summer sickroom opened and someone, anyone, even the doctor, meant comfort or loving-kindness or merely a distraction. Miss Cotterell had been aware of the girl when she'd come ashore – there was no other figure to be seen – a crouching shape bent to her task, her long red hair wound in a single plait, with a tangle of fishing nets drying around her. A busy little spidery thing with antic fingers, stitching and mending incessantly. She must have dreadful hands. She looked no more than twelve and already well used to it. Poor thing. Could that in any way be the sort of life she'd rather herself have had? Coarser but ruddier, stronger-limbed and -boned, one of let's say nine, all her days spent fetching and bearing, keeping the other children out of mother's way. Peering out at the same horizon waiting for the catch to come home, reading only the skies and the tides, or else, through the long fog-bound winter, wondering if the boats will ever return. Salt-wind whipping her hair. The serious, unlettered stare of penury. And nothing better than a world of far-fetched stories to believe in –sailors who came back rich and transformed to their womenfolk; whales the size of churches; the netted fish that sang in a girl's voice, a copy, they said, of hers, till they speared it for good measure.

Perhaps not. With no better end in sight, Miss Cotterell sets off towards her, telling herself not to put on airs, frighten the girl off. Shyness might be all they have in common, they come from such different worlds.

104

When she gets there, five yards or less from her, the girl is still wilfully holding her gaze, unsmiling. Miss Cotterell stumbles and blushes. What has she come all this way for? Is this some sort of game, some insolence, after all? The sun burns on her neck. The pitiful waves roll over. She begins to suspect a trap; she can sense her eyebrows knitting with suspicion. Close up, the girl's not half as grubby as she thought she'd be; her hair, though straggling, has a natural shine. And although she's thin, she's healthy-looking, must be at least fifteen.

'I see you've finished your mending.'

The girl nods, keeps her hands by her sides. Miss Cotterell could stand there wondering what they have to say to each other, but says,

'Looks like hard work.'

The girl blurts out, 'What I wanted to know more than anything, Ma'am, was what you sounded like...'

'I hope I haven't disappointed?'

'Nothing like me is what. I never really s'posed you would and now I'm right about it.'

'That's the sound of London you can hear. Not that everyone sounds like me,' she adds and treats the girl to her warmest smile. They seem baffled by each other's presence, though there must be more to tell. The blue and grey pebbles clack coldly like disparaging tongues whenever Miss Cotterell shifts her weight. She looks back to where the row-boat is safely beached. Mrs Pidgeon is certainly taking her time.

105

'I'm headed off to Italy. That's where we're going. My brother is waiting there for me. He assures me...'

She breaks off, feeling defeated. The girl seems to wonder at her.

'There are, he says, lemons ripening in February; the people there love to grow them in their gardens. The scent is overpowering.'

The girl takes a defiant breath. Is she even listening?

'Mother says I've not to talk to strangers, Ma'am. Nothing good will ever come from it, she says.'

'Ah, I see. I think it's a little too late to worry about that, don't you?'

The girl's shoulders let go of everything she's been holding back. She sinks down into the beach, tucks her heavy patched skirt under her knees, fiddles with her plait. Having checked the stones for weed and dryness, Miss Cotterell sits a little way off from her.

'She says you'll be putting wrong ideas in my head.'

Miss Cotterell hasn't lost the laugh she saves for friends. 'Isn't that what mothers are for?'

The girl returns a smile now. 'Is it true, Ma'am, in London, there are hundreds of ladies dressed in robes like only queens have, riding round and round on a track, but always sad?'

'It's not something I've seen myself.'

'But how's a lady live then? What can they find to do all day?'

What a strange loss Miss Cotterell finds herself at.

106

She wishes she'd stayed with Mrs. Pidgeon, who never asks her questions. But there's more:

'And can a girl, any girl, make shift for herself, do wonders there, in a place like that? What's there to learn about? If I got given money like theirs, could I do just what I'm minded to?'

'You could do all manner of things, I'm sure.'

At least the lie is an important one. And it's the one she knows so well. Brought up believing prettiness is a virtue. Grace a perfect curtsey. Her father, never insisting on any one point in particular, but never wrong, always more knowledgeable than her. Like her brother Charles, who could always come and go as he pleased.

'It's what I thought, Ma'am, though I know I've not to think it. It can't do much good.' She shakes her head, as if to clear it. 'That your ship out there, Ma'am, that's taking you far?'

Miss Cotterell nods, though doesn't turn to look. Out beyond the cove, the *Maria Crowther* is, like herself, doing nothing remarkable at all, creaking and sickening in all probability, stupefied and at anchor, nursing herself like the rest of them, licking her storm-wounds and awaiting worse.

'Do you know, I neither want to go on,' she hears herself say, 'nor shall I ever go back.'

* * * *

107

On the other side of the cove, Keats and Severn kick their heels amongst the stones; Severn is understandably trying his hardest. He could audition for an angel – he's so loyal, firm and true, has exactly the right kind of hair – if only he could keep his fears to himself.

'That songbird, can you hear it? Whatever it is, I say we'll be in Italy before it.'

Keats agrees to listen, cocks his head. There's a great deal to think about. When he doesn't reply, Severn tries again.

'Are you quite sure you don't want to go back?'

Why Severn persists with this line of thought, Keats doesn't know.

'I shan't change my mind.'

Severn guesses he's tiring his friend, but nevertheless goes on: 'In Biscay, it'll be too late, that's all.'

Keats knows his next line but won't say it. It's time to change the conversation.

'What I've been thinking about – and this will surprise you – is our dear Miss Cotterell. It's a shame she's not quite what you first thought.'

'What, my little Venus of Gravesend? I won't hear a word against her. She came through the storm and keeps herself, I think, remarkably cheerful.'

'Meaning I don't?'

Severn aims a pebble at his boots.

After an hour spent tramping the shelving beach,

littered with strands of amber-brown kelp and fractured shells of the same four types – mussel, cockle, razor and one they don't know curled like a gnarled toe – Severn calls a halt. He needs to sit down, but Keats is all for going on. Perhaps he has more on his mind. England has turned its back on him, banished him; will it try to prevent him even from straying on its beaches? Go on his way he will. When he looks back and sees Severn already leaning back on his elbows, unconcerned, busy admiring the rock-formations, he knows he's safe to emit a vanquished groan. With his genius for the private, Keats could hide almost any feeling from anyone, except his brothers. Except his jealousy. Except when phenomenally drunk. He picks up and whacks two flat white stones together for a while.

Afterwards, long afterwards, Severn will mistakenly recall only his own exhilaration on the shore, interpreting these strenuous walks as a sign of his charge's rude health, and not what they are – an attempt at self-destruction, a deliberate straining and weakening by Keats of his broken body. Later, this outing will come to seem a resounding success. Right now, out of reach, winded and sweating, Keats shrugs himself down on the stones, hugs his knees to his chest. A feint at tenderness. Shielding his eyes to stare at the scree of pebbles, he notices an unbroken razor shell, its perfect, picked whiteness emblematic of the sea's destruction, the shell opened up on its hinge, splayed and speechless. Neither echo nor song when he holds it to his ear. Just death strewn everywhere he looks, heaped in a two foot-wide ridge shucked and tossed up in an arc all round the cove.

Severn has stood up, is coming over. If he's quick, Keats should have just enough time before Severn catches up. The crunch of his steps will alert him. He disgorges his troubles in a fit of threats and curses. The surf sounds feebly to accompany him.

PART FOUR

The Sea

October 1820

England goes

For just a little longer, if he keeps on straining, England quails on the horizon. It seems to dawdle there, smudged and inglorious, just vestiges really, almost indistinguishable from murk, a grey veil of loss. Then it's gone, into the blue. When he's quite sure it's not coming back, Keats looks down at last, emptying his eyes out in the shifting surfaces of an unremittingly cold sea, waiting for his own reaction. Here comes misery, his old adversary, shouldering into him like a school ground bully. Surge after surge of it, unstinting, fills out his contours, all his muscles and nerves, describing him exactly, fulfilling wretched him. Poor John's a-cold. Orphaned again and for the last time, surely – what else

111

can be taken from him? – he thumps his fist at the rail, like a radical learning of some new injustice.

What's he left with this time? An insoluble Keats, a Keats in pieces, feeling cornered in mid-ocean, with only sea-level to look forward to: weeks of the curt horizon. Shitty ship's biscuit. Unwelcome companions, a crew that laughs at smut. All that he's leaving behind reaches out to him in one niggardly blow. He's cut off and trimmed away, like unsightly, marbling fat, from all he loves: heath and eglantine; oaks and aspens; tarrying Georgian girls, their compliant tresses coming languorously undone; a lonely walk all morning with nothing but poetry to spend his mind on. If his mind should start to mention names... In desperation, he alphabetizes types of suffering – anguish, black bile, caries, dearth... His one-time sorrow-charm, his rosary of words, is finally coming unstrung and useless now, beads trickling and scattering in every direction.

He knows he can't go on thinking like this. He longs for vacancy. How much finer it would be to lay down his thoughts like sheets of spotless linen, spread out to dry in enormous fields, end to end, just touching. Think of the sun's warmth throughout him down to the tiniest stitches.

But he can't. Can't but think of his illness, can't but go back to his betraying body. As soon as he reinhabits it, the shivers start up. He's forced to reacquaint himself with each symptom. His pulse races; he feels hectic, frantic, worn down. Not at all John Keats.

So which is worse? Thought or feeling? His body suddenly cricks and stoops him over, as if the mechanism had broken, funnelling everything that makes him him into a frown, a furrowed, founding-frown. No more memories, no more fancies, dreams. His wonderful, needle mind's reduced to a reflex brittle wince.

Like a banished queen, who has lost the love of her people, she refuses to watch her country disappear in the mist. She will not bow. Her guards let her be, downcast themselves: there's no pleasure to be had in confirming another's misfortune. Miss Cotterell shows as little as she can, her shoulders hunched. That's that, then. All that she loves recedes. Perpetual winter comes to Walworth...

How very different from the last time she went off on her own. She had escaped the house and all their eyes. Those delicious untold hours were all hers; she could be waylaid for as long as she pleased. She knew the way by heart, crossed the common just as she'd always done. This was the scene of her first disobedience, the one her father always alluded to when made sentimental by an evening's fireside quiet. Did she really, as he insisted she did, run away from everyone calling, calling, a little stray crouched in the bracken, learning the thrill of wrongdoing? No notion of time, back then. What she must have been like, elusive and fleet in the long grasses, smearing dirt on her cheeks and hands, happily ruining her nails. Was father's patience really tried so very often? What she remembers of him from then was a lenient, quiet man, tall and rough-cheeked, forever lifting her up and down again, tickling her under the chin. When he wasn't looking, she'd take off from him, sensing his absence, and would foray into the forbidden, some unexplored stand of trees or brambles requiring her attention. And no matter which wild flowers she brought back, it ended the same: summoned to a truth-telling with disappointed papa, his God-fearing hands behind his back.

All that happened long before her schooling in chores and curtseys began, before all those muted, scented conversations she'd had to have in every growing woman's proving-grounds, the host of drawing-rooms from Walworth to Dulwich. Hours of feints and parries with possible and impossible gentlemen, hours filled with the shows of surprise at what passes for wit and frankness in the suburbs. Her palette of blushes could be worked up into anything from meekness to outright consternation. She knew all the artful, darting glances that could bring about appeasement or leave a simple, trusting face crumpled with forlorn.

So it felt good to be alone. Quite without strictures, she made for the Old Kent Road, new foliage thrusting from the buds, gaiety itself pursuing her, on past the cherry trees, their exasperation at an unseemly, cold April unconvincing, given their frisson of blooms. *They* wouldn't be denied! Along the lane, there was nothing but a shambling dray, its driver sunk in some slovenly reverie. When she drew up alongside, marvelling at her speed and confidence, she hailed the man and the blinkered, winded mare looked up in astonishment

115

at the brightness of her voice. Summer pealed out of her. She could have been forgiven for thinking the afternoon sun, high and compassionate, cast more and more admiring looks her way, like her very own beau. Up there, the brisk resourceful blue kept on expanding, encouraging her steps. And for a long while she let herself know nothing, released into the breathless best of May, finding out for herself what it was to feel heartfelt again.

Within her, a silent working of wings trembled into being, a huge resplendent fie! to all the solemnity and sorrow of the previous few months. She forgot herself completely as she surefooted her way past the churchyard and rounded upon the village itself, taking it as if by surprise. Since it was neither market-day nor Sunday, she could have recited by heart what she expected to see. And how lovely – and amusing – to find the world – all Walworth – merrily going about its business without her. What she'd stopped picturing to herself in her invalid's room reeled around the green down there: an errand-boy lolling on a bench under the spreading beeches; well-dressed children out behaving, thinking about not muddying their shoes; someone in a frightful pother, stooping from his mount to ask directions; three young gentlemen lounging the afternoon through, unfairly apportioning a glazed pie bought fresh from Phelps'; a drunkard doing some complicated calculations with his fingers; four kinds of

116

smile as the well-to-do Dacres fell in with the well-to-do Shaws; the haberdasher's boy whistling up a ladder; the local prize-fighter swatting at flies; a Waterloo veteran with his chin sunk on his chest; the new governess she'd heard so much about, pocketing her spectacles; and somewhere, out of sight, the workhouse poor, only dimly aware of the day to be had outside...

It was precisely how muted, how misted, how insistently everyday the village seemed from up there on the common – the two rows of shops and houses smacked of anywhere – that made her stop and sink down, like that, in a swirl of skirts on a grassy bank. Her truancy had caught up with her. Life had gone on quite without her, and always would. She felt a tenderness rise up, a sorrow. Did no one in the village think of her? Petulance trembled on her bottom lip. Blood beat up into her temples, telling her she wasn't so nearly as well as she'd thought. On the point of a headache, about to droop down into herself, she spied the cleavers on her dress, sticky green burrs, the kind she'd played with years ago. By the time she'd picked them off, firing them one by one into the distance, she felt well enough, if not to continue, then at least to go back.

On her way home, birds she knew all about but couldn't see warned off others. In the lane, the pageant of lights and shadows grew ever more intricate. She'd stopped thinking about her setback. She was so pleased with herself at having avoided that horrid shower, sheltering under a great elm, she laughed and leapt at the puddles, skirting the clarts and slurps in which others less knowing would have got stuck above their ankles. Not her. There was a path she knew over there, a short-cut choked with nettles and cow-parsley that would be treacherous after rain like that. How right she was not to have taken it. Rest assured, she was coming back unscathed, elated and ever so good. She was coming back thinking of silliness and nothing much still; some surmises for the rest of the summer. She could afford them now, heedless in spotted silk underskirts, scarcely watching her step.

By the time she got back, father would be home, his worry turning the house upside-down, and the maid would be wringing her hands and most definitely for it. A full to-do, her father kindling, and then in she'd step, whole again, and the house would settle back, like a gate swinging to on its hinges. The maid would be reprieved, would shoot her perhaps a little black look, before taking up her work again. Miss Cotterell would make it up to her, with a bit of money. More importantly, left alone with father, already won round by her safe return, she'd have a whole afternoon to speak of, her own story to tell, charming him like she used to over supper, shining and companionable in his eyes, a reminder of her mother; he'd drink in her details like a lover. They'd share a splendid toast to her, make the evening linger, lighter, longer!

Instead, the maid was sent out to warn her. Where, where had she been? What was she thinking of? She'd been frantic, had looked the house over, thought herself about leaving for good, rather than face up to the master. No, he wasn't angry, but with something important to tell her, something, by the look of him, dreadful on his mind. She'd never seen him like this. Hadn't dared say a thing. A hundredweight of worries he must have; why, then, Miss, heap more on the poor man? Anyway she must come now, right away.

He was standing there in the parlour, white and leaking pain, the sharp edges of the heirloom clock behind him, its humourless face ticking her to task. His frame sagged terribly, as if unable to keep hold of the decision he had taken. It was something of great moment. Why else would he keep his head bowed for so long? She was stalled, held, a yard inside the door-frame, unable to go on. Her hand rose to her mouth. The other reached for something to lean against, but the door was behind her and she flailed there in a cruel space, receiving her sentence, awful noises coming from her.

How she refused. But it was true, it was true. She would leave for Naples at the end of the summer; Charles had kindly paid for her passage. She was inconsolable, her father's stiff comforting of her fruitless, till she accepted there was nothing left to show or be said. They sat there across the table from each other, severed. The twilight deepened between them. The clock sounded away. She was nothing to him; he was nothing to her. She felt her luckless skin shrivel. A blister swelled up on her heel. She got up to go to her room.

'I know what you're going to say,' she tried to begin, then stopped.

'Yes, yes you do, I'm afraid. My mind cannot be changed.'

'But have I no say in the matter?'

'No,' he said. 'No you don't. You have no say at all.'

As ever, her father's word was final, fatal, for the best.

Wave-forms: Resentment

He shouldn't be here. It shouldn't be him.

Knowing what he's thinking, the sea refuses to console.

Most of the time it's hushed, remote and alien. It's where the damned must go, endlessly laved and whirled, insufferably shriven, condemned to wash up on a dreadful shore; the sudden whitecaps not a mimosa flowering but a surge of protestation, rabid spittle, bubbling outcry of suffering and loss.

Or smooth for hours, fooling him, then smithereens, cracked mirror, needle-glints, salt-brittle, fractures that won't hold his gaze.

He shouldn't be here. It shouldn't be him.

It's full of vagaries, pointlessly sloshing its ill-will around. It hauls its morass, its shifting mis-shapes, nowhere at all.

Shouldn't, shouldn't.

Sometimes he can hear the strange cries it makes as it roils and churns, bleak in all directions. It looms idly, repeatedly, goes on widening, chastening, disinheriting.

A monstrous gullet, maw and rictus. Which gnaws at him.

With Fanny, April 1819

A little late morning skittishness, why not? Neither seems ready to object.

'It's entirely up to you, whether you choose to dote or not.'

He's already chosen, as she knows full well.

Unlikely, heady days, the two of them close-knit, up to love's no-good, sloping off unaccompanied to the Heath, carefree and sumptuous, twirling past Hampstead Ponds. Since the ground's hard enough after a dry spell not to splash their boots, they skirt the water's edge to the pinched alarm of the coots, then skitter down primrose slopes to this stretch only they know about, a bank so secluded Diana could be surprised there. The act of being together, unseen, makes it feel like an elopement. Their voices run and run through the woods. How many times has he made her laugh out loud? He swore he'd be impeccable, as soon as she asked him to be; as yet, she's asked for no such thing.

Wherever they look, summer reigns in spring. Leaves seem to unfurl for them. They duck under branches happy to oblige. The two of them feel like elaborate bows coming neatly undone. Here, far from prying eyes, from Fanny's mother's doubtful permission, from servants whispering in basement kitchens waiting for the loaves to rise, his head is full of her again and the make-do world seems a world away.

123

The arch of her foot has teased itself loose from its shoe. They are in danger of wantoning all afternoon. Keats talks up his prospects with a giddiness none of his friends has ever seen, swatting at his disappointments as if they were the summer's first dozing flies, knowing that at a particular look from her, designed to make light of him, he'll have promised away his life. She lets him go on, watching him dare to imagine a future with money. Any time now, she might feign a yawn or a swoon to ensnare him, make him wake or revive her with kisses. She loves nothing more than to prise him out of his book-talk – 'you and your eternal Dante' – nothing more than to smoke him out of his silent spells. What's a bookish fellow to do? He's told her all about Paolo and Francesca, and still she doesn't care! She is both pepper on his tongue, and a cellarful of the best claret, cooled.

'And if this gentleman of means, handsome, tall, correct and so on, should dare to ask for her hand too soon?...'

She leans back, holds up her nails and smiles.

Who's known foolhardying like it, amongst such culpable trees, whose low branches, just coming into leaf, abet them? The marvellous full boon of her – perplexing, provoking and then as plain as you like – delights and lightens him. She maddens him out of himself and when all he has to choose between is the bullish introspection he's always fallen back on or this

124

turbulent, truculent thing, this feeling...

For the first time, Keats finds he can fill hours swapping ridiculous dares that always end with the same forfeit. It's her self-sufficiency that takes him aback; she's adamant she can take him or leave him; she much prefers novels; she won't stand for inspiring a single line from him. At one point, he hears her draw back the hammer of the duelling-pistol and realizes he isn't, after all, going to flinch. And the smoke isn't ever going to clear and the report will be deafening. He'll handsomely submit, then stagger back yards, stricken and clutching at his chest, though his second and the doctor present will never find the ball or the wound. She simply has him in her thrall:

'I swear,' he says, 'if you let me love you, I will never unhand you again.'

'O to be hand-in-hand with my all-in-all.'

It's only when she talks about her dog, how she snuggles up to him at night, that Keats first feels troubled. A snug stone thrown in the pond drops like a jealous pang. The ripples make off as though from some misdemeanour. All his feelings emanate from her.

Later that night, after a little composition, he gives himself over to ravenous re-assembly, making her again in his mind, tinkering with all her known, and unknown, proportions. And to think, she's just the girl next door. As simple as that. After all the wondering, all the refusing to believe. Like him, tonight, she will be

125

lying awake, beyond that damnable partition wall, their faces turned in the same direction. They've made a pact to draw the curtains, blow out the candle, and direct their prayers for each other, at precisely the same time. Cloud willing, they'll have wished upon the same bright star. If he could, he'd co-ordinate their breathing, oversee their heartbeats, harmonise their roaming fancies in their sleep. He wishes her sweet dream-assignations, all love's licence to explore.

Bad symptoms

They come on her like a sudden soot fall, smothering everything. She has to save what she can before the house and all its furnishings – those expensively upholstered chairs, that richly detailed carpet – are ruined. Her head swims. She can scarcely breathe. She blinks at the damage being done to her. When she tries to straighten her fingers, she can't; the whole of the last wasted year balled up in her fists.

Occasionally, she hears voices:

'How is she now?'

'Poor thing, poor thing.'

She knows they're talking about her, whoever they are, until she's suddenly gone again; pale, hot head against the pillow, her body mere bulges under a sheet, her breathing slowed and shallow. She just lies there, like a jack that won't go back in its box, good for nothing.

There are days like this when she seems barely alive. Empty coal-scuttle. She faints for up to four or five hours at a time, as if drugged. Sweet, sedate dreams she won't remember. Would it have been so very unforgivable to have sauntered, arm in arm, with her friend, the night glazed over with stars, down into the furthest shadows? The moonlight would have been her judge. Off the gravel paths he would have led her, into tenderness. No quandaries, no silly breathy qualms. There she would have stood, as expectant and as still as any country girl, seizing on her chance. And then, greedy, voracious, not caring if she frightened him with her appetite, biting his trembling lip.

No poetry and no sleep

At least it's no worse at night. Keats coughs as quietly, as selflessly, as he can. A little moonlight and he can make out the caulking if he stares long enough. That's what boats are made of. He tries to make sense of the knots and swirls above his bunk. See things. Take comfort from them. He sees, for certain, tidal patterns, drooping eyelids, frowns; ripple-rings from a steady, unnerving drip; swollen nodes; an open vulva; attenuating candle-flame; a slanted death's head. Below him, the even breathing that he envies most of all: Severn no doubt dreaming of unlimited canvas stretching all the way to Rome. Behind the curtain, the occasional collapsed whinny of Miss Cotterell in some school-girl distress; Mrs Pidgeon in a wilful silence, severe as a winter river, full of grey asperity.

One thing's for certain, he won't take up the pen. His once-brilliant mind, so conspicuously trained, his veal-brain so sumptuously fed, won't for a minute consider it. Yes, it thrives, turning him over and over, till he thinks himself out of all proportion. Even memories turn on him: simple things he took for granted hindsight complicates. Some words won't ever let him go. Conversations he meant in his head to be fond and forgiving, turn poisonous, garrulous, fraught with tension: why didn't he say more in the time he had – or less? Why didn't he, once and for all, get the right redress, leave his lover in no doubt? Or should that have been more doubt?

He wipes his hand up and down the waxy feel of his face. The greasy patina that comes off on his fingers reminds him of cold chicken. What he would like to have in mind are knife-edges of light, sweet clarities, images seen in the most advantageous colours. He wants to stand back and admire the gloss, his fat clay pots happily dribbling whitewash, the telltale brushes in his hand.

Low point

'Severn!'

A hiss in the dark. It takes all the despair he can muster, reaching out, unmanned like this, towards a comfort that will only heap up shame. Bleak need makes him croak: 'Severn!' Carelessly, compulsively now, he leans over the edge of the bunk, his old man's hand starting to flail.

Severn's wrapped in some dream of acclaim, all rightfully, finally his. He's been bowing and bowing in a great Italian hall, Rococo-style, accepting the applause and has acknowledged at least three academicians and recognised a score of friends, their upturned, ravished faces. His mother and sister look out exultant from exactly where he knew they'd be...

'For God's sake, Severn!'

But Severn won't let go of his reward, his time in the chandelier light, his bask in the radiant palace of promise met. Cherish it, cherish it, he seems to snort to himself, harrumphing his right shoulder away. But already the glow is going, the murmurings sound fainter, less certain, there's a persistent cracked and critical voice coming from somewhere he can't place. Who can it be who can't wait? Where, come to think of it, is his father? His eye grows ever more clouded, ever more roving... Doubtfully, reluctantly, he has to come back to the heavy sea sway, to his sickbed hell, to the interminable

131

ragged pitch and creak and this time, to something else, something withered and frantic, scratching at his cheek.

'Good God, Keats! Keats, is that you?'

Keats daren't open his mouth, for fear of what might come out. Whimpers, impieties, globs of blood. A lunatic's gibber. He prods at Severn one more time, then collapses back on his pillow and waits while his breathing comes back to him, raspy and runaway. By the time Severn has come back to himself, calling sleepy, stock-in-trade sympathy up through the bunk, Keats has stiffened with decision, as if injecting himself with cold. Severn's face eventually glides into view; pummelled with bad sleep, still at his queasy stomach's beck and call, he's nevertheless as ready to oblige as ever. But it's what Keats looks like that's the problem: two wild white eyes that can't focus, like a cow's at the shambles, and a pinched, wrecked countenance, glistening with sweat, that gleams like a wrinkled death-mask. His teeth can't stop chattering. He looks like he could sheer in two, like an overheated iron plunged in the water barrel. The mouth hole moves; he speaks in dry gasps.

'Medicine-box. Get me the medicine-box.' These syllables sound like poured sand. A mendicant's eyes implore Severn. 'I can't take it. The key. Get me the key to the box.'

Severn blinks, still half-stunned by his dream.

'Are you sure this can't wait till morning?' Why he asks this, he has no idea.

132

'Do I look like it can wait? Do as I ask and get me the box.'

Severn ruffles his face. These are not the right questions, not the right answers. He stands his ground, frowning like a misled child.

'Are you quite all right?'

'What do you think?' Keats' hoarse, defiant roar comes out. 'The pain comes on like a spear thrown in up to here.' He tugs at the loose skin at the base of his throat. The gesture, or the image, seems to work. Severn is wide awake now, unconsciously rolling his sleeves.

'Be calm, be patient. I know what you want. Where is the pain this time?'

'Where it's always been. Throughout me. Everywhere defining me. And the key?'

'In my trunk. Or should be. To be honest, I haven't bothered looking since Portsmouth.'

A further spasm sends Keats deep into silence. He is seized by the dark all around him, as if by the scruff.

'My God, John, are you sure – whatever it is that's wrong – are you absolutely sure it can't wait?'

Yes, Keats is bloody well sure. His grimaces say as much. Something in him that seems cornered and blood-flecked, forces Severn to hurry up and take stock. He ducks down and is gone a long time. More dark swims in. Keats can hear him rummaging and fumbling about. A conscience's tussle. None of which is helping.

133

When he resurfaces, panting like a pearl-diver, holding the key, he's dispensed with his good humour, has returned wearing earnest. This is not good, and will not lead to good. Severn has more than an inkling now of what Keats is after and has come back armed with all the orthodoxy he can muster. He's been preparing himself for this, though he's only just realized it. What Keats wants is to die. And die now. There's laudanum enough. Quickly, peacefully, in one sinful, heavenly dose. And Severn has no intention of letting that happen. This is the growing conviction that has calmed and fixed him; a sour, sure caution puckers his lips. He has determined to lengthen his pauses, make the night work with him, delay him till dawn when the others wake up, look around, stretch a little, carry on being. There is still succour to be given. Though not sure how to begin, Severn looks almost inspired for a moment, ready to dispense all the good sense he has. Keats sees straight away that he has been intercepted, interpreted. The game is up; the cup and dice fall from his hand. He claws at the sheets, seething that he's been so easily discovered. He was always cleverer than this.

'This pain you have – insufferable and unspeakable as it is – you have to accept...'

Keats interrupts, villainous with resolve.

'I accept nothing. Nothing as it is. Nor did I ever. That's what made me me.'

'But you have to accept that at certain times...'

134

'For God's sake, Severn, I said I won't. I won't, you hear. You know who I am, as well as any other. You know full well how this will end. We both do. I know it infinitely better than you and yet you deign, you dare...'

'Where you're going, John, unless I'm grievously mistaken, is Italy. Our Grand Tour of sorts, remember. And if you're thinking of taking heaven by surprise like this, I'm afraid you're not going there, not yet. When you do, it will be when He sees fit and no sooner and I won't have a hand in your rashness. What you're contemplating is wrong and you know it. All this is just the despair in you speaking. It's your soul I'm thinking of...'

'You don't know what thought is. Look at me, a sorry, wasted stick. That's the body of a man who's thought things through. What I've thought, what I know, is that I don't want to go on. You've seen with your own eyes what I've gone through. I've seen you look away. If I expectorated any harder the soul you talk about would fly out at once. We were not meant to suffer like this; it is not set down in any book to be like this.'

Keats is talking himself round and out, and hates himself for doing so. Only the words are doing his dying now. Severn says nothing, waiting for the abatement. Silence is his form of bloodletting.

'So you say you won't help me, though you see how I suffer.'

'No, I won't.'

135

'Though you see how it destroys me, you can stand there and say you will not help.'

'In this I will not help you, no, though in all other things I will care for you as though for myself.'

'As though for myself.' Keats sinks back in the sweat of the vanquished. He shuts his eyes. His throat burns. His mien has completely gone, his dignity shot to pieces. He lies there working his mouth in silent laughter. Denied. He tries to lick his crusted lips, then lies back down in the caul of his death-wish. Resignation shivers through him like expelling a black, recalcitrant stool.

'You could at least make yourself useful and get me some water. Then put out the candle. I've done.'

Mrs Pidgeon's up before the others, annoyed with herself. There's nothing to be gained from losing her temper. She, more than any of them, must remember her comportment. Hourly she thinks of it, castigates herself. More than any of them, she has the strongest stomach, the will. What she lacks in money, family, she can more than make up for in rigour. But staying seemly isn't as straightforward as it looks. Ships were not built with ladies in mind. Only a shabby curtain to get dressed behind. She worries constantly about what she's let slip.

Day after day, she stares at the same predicament: what to do with herself, what to do about herself. Day after day, the same succession of dirty clouds shoulder-charging the sky, threatening, the sea continuing rough. It's true the girl means well, but she wants too much. All Mrs Pidgeon has to offer – common-sense, forthrightness – must seem like crow's comfort. Practical, that's all she is, and practical's not enough. Not when she can hear Miss Cotterell crying herself to sleep at night.

In truth, she's waiting for a change, a leak of light, some kindness in her to find its way out; she longs for the clouds to break, one way or the other: storm or bright sun. Put an end to the way things are: judgement days, one after the other, in every one of which she's been found wanting. Who's she got that she can tell this to? God hears her silent prayers, yet can do nothing to prevent her growing waspish, spoiling to morose.

She is curtailed.

What of it?

She shouldn't be so hard on herself. How often must any ship – even the rankest, the most rotten, the most deservedly written off – right itself in the worst of storms? Just so long as it's seaworthy. She must see that. All this morbidity calls for more fortitude; a truce with the worst of her thoughts.

Up in the rigging, partially obscured, one of the crew will be harbouring uncharitable thoughts about her, watching her humour wrinkling and pursing. No, she can't help herself. She can shrug her shoulders all she likes, vow to make amends, wrap her blue shawl determinedly about her, none of it will help her to become any more becoming. Sadly, there's not enough of it in her nature. She's getting more and more like her husband was, when he came back from the war. How did that go again? A few weeks of his pained accepting of her, then an odd stillness about him, bursts of exasperation. She soon stopped worrying at him. He'd spit on the floor and stare, not even studying his drink, mouldering in memories he couldn't share. There was no understanding him. No matter what she said, a torpor hung about him; he stirred his crutch in little circles, staring at the motes, wishing days would get themselves

138

over with. Before long, he had the stupid, rheumy eyes of a man in retreat, outmanoeuvred. She learned to avoid catching his eye. He stayed all day by the grate, watching it go cold, refusing to tend it. A rotting, upturned hull in its own foul weather. To keep the two of them, she made herself useful to others, worked all hours; made sure she wasn't there, had no wish to be, the day he got up and disappeared for good. No one talked about him afterwards. She just got on with things. Did so then, will do so again.

Or else, if she's not careful, she'll end up like him.

139

Reclining chair

Furious in his greatcoat, clenching his bird's-feet hands in his pockets, fathoming nothing, Keats makes the salt air crackle, back off. He's worse than before, again, shrunk to the merest speck of mind. If only it would vanish, leave him be completely. But that consternation in the muscles flares up; his throat prickles and roughens, feels full of tiny bristles, like the underside of a nettle-leaf. A cow's eyelashes. The edge of the stable door rubbed over and over by the horse's neck, stretching for its fair share of feed. The mule brays when it won't go any further, sensing danger, desperate to impose its will. A packhorse might snort and rear out of terror on the mountain pass. What words will be left *him* to say? What possible sounds will remain? He recalls his father's screams – whatever happened to the horse that threw him, that made everything wrong from the start? – but that was a violent sudden death. This one, his own, will have been with him, holding his hand, for some time. Can't keep its hands off him. Practically rubbing its hands to receive him. Perhaps a murmur will escape him. When the time comes, he hopes Severn will be listening, pencil at the ready, to embellish it.

Why is he still here? Static stalks him warily. Gulls keep their distance; Severn's soft pencil sketches ever more quietly. Keats looks up from his pretence at reading. It is unspeakable, what we expect from the

140

heart. Poor scuffed valiant thing. His chest tightens to remind him of what he had, still under the haunt of her. To have been in her arms, full of faith, her eyes stilled in shadow and certainties and to know she'll be visiting town by now, looking in shop windows with friends, tattle-telling...

Clinker-build your heart, John Keats, caulk yourself against its seeping sentiments, tar its whorish pores. It's worth returning to that bed-ridden May, a year on from his Odes, when his turn of phrase had become vinegary and inveighing. Against birdsong; strong light; twilight; the blackest night; against armies of quacks, fool-parsons, and apothecaries; against town; against the country, the country that harboured him. The sheer inchoate noise of his ailing, his machinations, embarrassed him. How did poor Tom ever manage it, dying in a frightened peace, just nineteen? Where did he, a mere boy still, no older than Miss Cotterell, learn quiet like that? That wan impenetrable smile he had, his extraordinary answer to everything, right until the end.

Two of the crew are moistening lines, fashioning fish-hooks and barbs. They sit cross-legged in their happiness, crafting and thinking ahead. Something down there is swimming moonily around, unprepared for the sudden hoist, the violent hefts, the life-or-death struggle. And what would these men do, if they pulled up a fat, unknown catch, its big lips working in horror, its glutinous eyes beseeching them? Wouldn't they throw it

141

back in disgust, smear their hands on their thighs and try to forget it? That catch is what Keats sees, when he shuts his eyes; he sees the worst. Through a bedroom wall, he hears the clamours and wails of those he's left behind, a dearly-loved daughter clinging to her mother, her hands punching at the wronging air. What's the use of seeing that? What kind of insight does that bring? That could be *anyone's* sense of loss! These shadow-figures make all the gestures of mourning, say the right things to each other through their tears, show their resolve to go on living without him. They know it's what he would've wanted. But when he tries to tell them no, that's not what he wants at all, when he tries to tap them on the shoulder, turn them round to let them know he's there, they have no faces, their flesh is blurred, their lips are thin and blue, they gape at nothing.

He considers other nightmares too: a recurring one has Fanny continually vanishing down an enticing hedgerow walk. Where the shadows take her remains obscure. He has not earned that privilege. The bad dream affords him a close scrutiny of her nape, the spring in her ringlets, as slow summer air plays on her stray hairs; he admires the fine down on her cheek. His thoughts pluck at the soft, loose ribbon around her waist. A glimpse of pale, remembered calves. She is forever sidelong now, with the ghost of a smile; he can clearly see the quiver of her eyelashes, can nearly trace her clavicle. The tilt of her head shrugs him off – 'not till we're married' – before

142

she moves off. It's at this point he gets to his feet, calling, then realizes he can't keep up; his sea-legs taunt him as he stumbles after her, and when he wonders what's the matter with him, looks down to see he's been hobbling on two blistered, suppurating stumps.

By day, the hours won't fill up. Level emptiness extends in all directions. Back he goes, to the dark last resort of himself, the familiar razed plain. From where he stands, he can pick out fallow fields, signs of abandoned settlement. No undulation. He sees himself as Lent; a handful of withered apples in a barrel; the last of the salt-pork; a jar of bitter pickles. The hoard he once had – not for sharing – now exhausted. He is simply cargo, freight, passage paid.

Him and his hodge-podge thoughts. Wasn't he just thinking he's lost his one and only minx, lithe and lovely-teasing in her complexity, her changeability? He has built a shrine to love so secret and obscure, so private and remote, he's lost his own way there. He is cursing, slashing through the undergrowth. Its marble slab and columns are choked in brambles, couch-grass and bindweed, whose white trumpet flowers seem an ironic taunt. No one goes there now. Now, though he's shown it no one, he holds the cold cornelian she gave him to remind him of how it cooled their fingers, when she nursed him through that hot spell. A cursed, reverse Pygmalion: all the thrilling surfaces of her, all her tensions, recast to a mottled marbled keepsake.

143

Wave forms: Regret

The choppiness seems to be relenting. Even waves tire. They slacken off, appeased for now, seem more convivial, though their bluster and their playfulness have gone.

What remains is rue, rue, unruly rue.

Of course he should have had her when he was in health. Worse, he had the occasions. At least three or four times, after dark in Well Walk, he could have endeavoured to, before she came to mean too much to him. Flushed from their daylong skirmishing, the night air still highly scented, still warm and agreeable, that pressure from her palm and that loose laugh of hers, now he recalls and recalls it, were obviously an invitation. The Heath was in swooning distance, the two of them already out later than they'd promised...

Or what about when he came back from Dorset, his mind set on her, tingling at the one thought of her, ready to press his advantage home?... But then her mother had delayed and delayed her errand, sensing something reckless about him.

And in any case, there was always the wretched small talk to be got through, his own sickly wavering, his fear lest some fateful servant, some fraught messenger, nose pressed against the pane when no one answered, might somehow...

Of course, he should have had her.

In truth, he thought too highly of her to desire her in that way.

Of course, he should have had her.

So now there are just pictures of her, frenzied guesses: how she might have lain there, coiled, lithe, unhurried, or coy and concealing; gleaming, candlelit, thrilled, straining and eager-obvious, or else ethereal, subtle-supple, mistily bedewed; now crude and whisper-willing, strong-muscled, adamant and yielding; sometimes faux-reticent, sometimes girded, rippling, fluted; first enabling, then ennobling, wonder-wreathed, agog; or even sobbing, horribly undone; unleavened, risen; wonderfully drowsy, creamily cool; pensive, pursed and yet pursuing; unbidden and all-encompassing; so very milky-white, almost mauve; emboldened on occasion; on occasion so wild, though gratefully snared, bared, completely discovered...

Round and round, the cold cud of if only. He can't keep any of it down. Not to be swallowed, like a spendthrift's laughter caught in a miser's throat. He seems doomed

145

to replay it now, endlessly circling, improving... For a minute, he senses they're alone together, in her room next door, and she calls his name out in a voice he's never heard before, hoarse with tenderness, but he won't answer, his mind patching and stitching like never before, pausing foolishly for thought, before coming away empty-headed, but she's still there, reaching for him and calling him back, he's opening the door and once again, they're alone together, in her room next door and she calls...

And so on.

It's him, of course it is. *He* is the banished hectic, suffering his insights, drenched in his night-sweats, buffeted between what he thought were safe shores. His blasted heath's the Atlantic, beset by prevailing winds, gunning from the south west, accusing and tormenting him. This cabin's the squalid hut where he must examine himself and rage against the elements. Trials all day long in his head.

The talented Severn can play either Kent or Gloucester. His choice.

Mrs. Pidgeon and Miss Cotterell will stand in for the women who have turned against him.

And no, he will not be preached to, least of all by her, pretty head bowed before her New Testament. If she dares to try and comfort him that way again, persuade him from his Shakespeare, these are the passages he'll show her. She won't come back in a hurry.

1   As flies to wanton boys are we to the gods; they kill us for their sport.

2   Give me an ounce of civet, good apothecary, to sweeten my imagination.

3   Hysterica passio! Down, thou climbing sorrow, thy element's below.

4 Thou art a boil a plague sore in my corrupted blood.

5 The wrathful skies gallow the very wanderers of the dark.

6 O I have ta'en too little care of this.

7 It is the stars, the stars above us govern our conditions.

8 Give me thy arm: poor Tom shall lead thee.

9 If I were your father's dog you should not use me so.

And, doubly underlined in soft pencil, with an asterisk beside it:

10 Man's nature cannot carry th'affliction nor the fear.

Death by drowning

As a matter of interest, what's to prevent him *at any time* from simply tipping himself over, spilling himself clumsily like the contents of a jar? Is it plain fear? Thoughts of poor Severn left with long letters of expiation to write? Cowardice and honour, that outmoded pair? There must be some dormant duelling-instinct in all young men fending off the longing for death. Perhaps Keats has a talent for withstanding. His mind adjusts itself daily, somehow takes care of him. Like an exorbitantly-oiled yet stuttering mechanism, it countenances new suffering, attains another level altogether of hardship and loss. The noises it makes, the complaint! He's not happy with the accommodations he's made with pain. How did he learn to do that? Not, like Miss Cotterell, through the example of Christ. If he thought that, then he'd stride over aft and lever himself right over *without thinking*. And therein lies the difficulty, there's the notorious rub.

Now would be perfect. No, now *is* perfect. Now, when everyone else is about their useful, necessary tasks, washing or muttering or praying, he could slope over in all innocence and cleverly tumble free. As quiet as a sigh escaping. All he need do, if challenged, is to intimate he had a mouthful of spit he needs to send over the side. A criminal's craft skulks in us all.

But whenever he contemplates the drop, and the

149

impact it would have, he knows he never will. At what appears such a long way down, the waters wrestle and fret in their ages-old tussle, a host of mean, old whitebeards squabbling over who owns what, characteristically refusing to let him see into anything. No future down there, no answers, just endless dissolution.

Besides, what kind of man willingly sucks in his death, swallowing it whole, his mouth wide open on purpose though looking as if taken by surprise? It would require iron deliberation, a surge of rank unhappiness. It strikes him as abhorrent, absolutely against nature. How would he still his thrashing legs, feeling the cold course through him, filling his pockets, checking him with its ruffian hands for coins and rings? Rifling his memories, turning him outside in? Others had done it, of course, felt the sun going out of their bodies, quenched in a single breath. They had what it took, though they kicked out instinctively like a foal, while their hearts fought for rich, airy blood. But what extremes did they have to feel, to let go like that? How could anyone snap shut a lifetime's urges and wiles, like a disagreeable book, relax the throat muscles sufficiently coolly to take another draught, willing more deadweight down into their lungs, guts, thighs? He lacks the deep calm, or disarray. Besides, knowing his luck, they'd have a rope thrown out and around him in seconds, his body popped up by an unforeseen bubble, gulping and pawing weakly at the uncomprehending air, saved from himself.

150

Much of the morning can be whiled away thus in gentle distraction, skirting temptation, letting these thoughts press down on him, like thumbs into an orange. Theorising does him the power of good. This way of thinking's a prop to him, if anything. He can bruise himself with his black philosophy all day long and Severn will never guess or see his way to meddling.

So what *is* stopping him, if, as he's conceded, there's no retrieving the past? What keeps him drumming his fingers, turning things over, making the odd cheering remark? Could it really be *her*, Miss Cotterell? No attraction, just affection. Could it be as simple as that? He can't think of much else to look forward to. Italy is losing its appeal: all that paperwork and days of travelling on dreadful roads. It *must* be her, sicklier than ever, her discreet cough persisting. Hearing her worsen, he's grown as fond of her as of a reflection. Her case is desperate; that alone helps to rally him. That, and his determination to outlast her.

151

Reading matters

Today, the mild light is kind on the eyes. No one mentions the sea. They are cosily ensconced, all in their rightful chairs. At her recommendation, Severn is galloping through one of Miss Cotterell's adventure novels, translated out of the French. It's powerful, unsubtle stuff, a determined assault with all the siege-guns of Romance. Stuff that he's not really ready to engage with. Extreme sensibility. When he surreptitiously skips ahead, he finds the same characters in strikingly different scenes – balconies, battlements, a peasant's cottage in the woods – but with exactly the same feelings they had and still talking too much. Of course, he'll tell her what she wants to hear; yes, she's right, it is *truly* unbelievable. Remarkably so. But though he keeps his place with her bookmark, and wonders what it must have put in her head, he's no longer inclined to read between the lines, not inclined that way at all. Cured, as a matter of fact, of any fancies of that sort which he might have had. That storm went out of its way to administer him a vigorous, corrective slap. He reads, and sees, differently now.

Yawning, after a while, he looks up at the others, still immersed in their books and smiles sadly to himself. Keats is biting his lip; appreciatively, Severn assumes. The turned page sounds like a clean slice through an onion. Mrs Pidgeon is the odd one out, furthering her embroidery. She's got as far as a tangle of green stems

152

that still want flowerheads. She is saving the petals till last. Otherwise, they seem like a well-to-do family in an open-air drawing-room or on an outing, respecting each other's silences: they have thoroughly domesticated the deck.

'I find it helps to turn the pages slowly on days like this, don't you?' he says, but doesn't really want a reply.

Keats is giving his copy of Byron filthy looks. Like everyone else, he finds he has to keep on dosing himself with his words. What infuriates him is that the man's daring succeeds. Think of the staggering sales his Lordship commands and all because of his soiled name. Fame stinks, truly, its rot sniffed at by the crowding thousands who judge its perfume troubling, sweet and fine. At least Keats acknowledges it won't get a fair reading from him. He can't turn the page without another gnawing flash. And light reading was meant to be good for him, was supposed to quieten him down. He can't afford the best emotions, let alone envy's ingenious poisons. But on he scours, looking to quibble wherever he can, looking out for a mishandling of tone, a predictable end-rhyme. He holds the volume at the ends of his knees, ready to take offence, like a firebrand waiting to fly up at a perceived slight. He's made it clear to Severn that his antipathies for Byron have nothing to do with women. How, despite his club foot, does he create a steady swoon amongst lovely, clever ladies who ought to know better? He stirs their longings.

153

Apparently, whenever his carriage passes by, in well-to-do breasts countless hitherto unknown feelings throng to him, determined to develop into heartache, heart murmurs, heart-flutterings for the rest of their lives. Ah, well. Whereas obscure, quaint Keats has always been left alone to beetle about in obscurity. Counting his pennilessness. How can one way with words be worth so much more than another? When he reaches the part where the shipwrecked passengers tuck into their cannibal feast, which isn't in the least bit funny, he's read enough. There's only one thing for it, and without a backward glance:

'Help! Ho! Help! Lordship overboard!'

Severn loves to see him like this, better again, loves him without a doubt.

The bellying of the sail

Despite the onset of everything, the two of them, starved of home-affection, have come to recognise what they have in common. There's no danger in shared circumstance. Miss Cotterell likes to listen to what Keats has to recount. Men have such fuller lives. Still, this is one thing to be thankful for, the two of them standing here, feeling the new breeze in their drawn faces, looking up at the sails.

The first lean tremor of wind, a tic of north-north-east, brings a steadier pulsing in the topsail. A flicker of ripples leads to an unmistakeable tautness, to the whole extraordinary filling out, the unfurling into strength, vitality, a great, glorious, white-sheeted convalescence, yards of patched-up sailcloth snapping into satisfaction, big with self-display. Fruitfulness, annunciation. Muscling, white, clarion roar.

She turns to Keats to verify something.

'You know what your friend said to me, on our first morning at sea, off Ramsgate, when the wind was strengthening? He said a full sail's a courting sail, harnessing the wind's caresses.'

Keats blushes on Severn's behalf. 'That doesn't surprise me. You've noticed, I take it, how enthusiastic he can get? Sometimes he says things he shouldn't.'

'Ah, that's what I'd thought.'

155

Wave-forms: Indifference

The same stretch of sea bounds on in precisely the same way, like somebody else's well-trained faithful dog she can't shake off, panting, following her every move, but not heeding her, performing no tricks at all, retrieving nothing.

For all she cares, they can veer endlessly into the dreaded and sheer; off-course, on-course, none of it matters.

The winds shift easily, trying to flatter, but Mrs Pidgeon won't look up there any more; clouds can build all they like, or fizzle and taper; a sea-bird can stay loyal if it so desires, hankering after something, following them for days, so what if it does? Mere instinct.

She is carrying a tray of thoughts piled so high, like sophisticated tea-things, fine-bone-china'd, so high she can't really see in front of her, and the tray is very heavy lately, on the point of tipping, slipping from her grasp, and she can see, before it happens, the shock of the shards sliding across the floor, the abject apology she must make to all her guests.

She finds herself in an at-home without refreshments, without music or intrigue or the slightest amusement, from which she is forbidden to leave.

Another storm is massing on the horizon. The swell comes on apace. None of them can afford to lighten or loosen or lessen.

A Salve, of sorts

For once, there's a favourable breeze; Severn is up on deck, gladly losing track. He sits there, nodding at the south and drifting along more serenely than any vessel, entertaining a time – not too distant, he'd like to think – when he's got his hands on fabulous wealth. He listens to the bright chink of his daydream, drowsing through its dazzle. In this state of mind, he finds words can come loose, get freed up from their usual meanings, their moorings; such a word, say, as tiptop. Tiptop. Tiptop. See? Or, and he likes this one, alights on this one – shipshape. Shipshape. Shipshape. Shipshape. Shipshape. Say it often enough and he could end up believing all's well.

Some consternation in the sails disturbs him, rounds on him; he goes back to the scene of the most recent storm, Mrs Pidgeon's part therein. Could she really have meant what she said? Words like that can't have come easily to her. And yet he saw the astringent face she pulled when she couldn't bear it any more, the tendons in her neck about to snap as if she'd set herself – eyes, teeth and every tensing muscle – against the elements, as if she were a sea-hag grappling with a fiend. No, too fanciful, Severn. Though if fiend it was, she was fighting something already in her. After all, they'd all feared for their lives that night, yet no one else had surrendered so completely.

158

There are some natures, he supposes, which on finding themselves in constantly superior company – one more tolerant, another more stoical and the other strangely with greater piety and zest – cannot help but spit out accusations and black suspicions or turn an innocent remark into an unforgivable slight. Such natures, when pushed to the extreme, only seek out further blight.

What was said has certainly made for some unpleasantness. There *should* be some redress, he fancies. Keats said he'd have no more of her, said he hated her type; just shut his eyes again. But he's not what he was. What's to be gained from settling back down to seethe against her? Why scratch at the rash and make it worse? Someone will once again have to apply the salve. Severn's famous balms and ointments.

He must think this through properly. Despite what Keats said – 'rumination makes for ruination' – there's little else to do. All this sizing up and circling round can make a man seem wiser than he is. The problem is how to rein thoughts in. They flit about, not exactly out of anxiety, but just because they're there. No way out for any of them. He's started to feel something of what the unfortunately-married man must feel, after a tremendous, hurried courtship – plenty of time, sea-acres of it in fact, in which to know better.

They should have thought harder, taken stock, all of them. And he, he of all people, so easily swayed, so tender in his consideration of others, should have done some downright useful considering for once. He knows where he's going with this: Rome. It's Rome that's to blame. If it hadn't been for Rome having been dangled before him, spinning like a crystal on a chain...and he'd grabbed at it like a boy, like a credulous... And now fancy that: what looked a miracle turned out a mirage.

Guess what? He's done it again! Hurrah for Joseph Severn, slopping weak poison into his own ear! So much for resolution. He was supposed to be resolving Mrs Pidgeon, not revolving round... Plate-spinner! With that, he flips open his pad and sketches for a long, long time, sizing up the play of lines and sails, shading in. Keeping his hand in and his mind out. Occupied again.

He has no idea how much later it is when he hears the last thing he wanted: Mrs Pidgeon's stout ascending. She puffs and blows like an ill-fated porpoise, filled with foul purpose. She *can't* want to harry him now. He has nothing prepared! Surely she'll simply acknowledge him, take her turn in the air and there'll be no more said.

She heads for him straightaway. Now is as good a time as any. She must press on; she has been exercising her right to resentment ever since the storm. Obedient, it runs along beside her, its blistered tongue lolling out of black gums, no wag in its tail anymore. No, she has nothing to reproach herself with, though he sits there with his scribbles as if she hadn't just now emerged.

160

Why are men like this? Always seeming to be doing. Taking themselves up to some higher ground they want everyone to notice they've established. Oh they will have talked about her between themselves, she can be sure of that, refining their objections. Dipping their sermonizing buckets in some special well of theirs. She's felt them disregard-regard her, turning up their noses at her as though at a basket of spotted brothel-linen. She knows there's little chance of undoing her undoing; they have set her where she must stay forever, at the mercy of decorum's absolute no-quarter. Did she really think any of her how-to-begins she'd rehearsed would help? No, what she wants is to have this out. This is the only way she's ever known – bristling forward, seeing the doubts scatter.

As she comes up, her shadow cuts across Severn's mock concentration and settles, as if unsure whether to hover or loom, but either way forcing him to engage with her.

'They're fast asleep, the pair of them,' she says, determined to install herself. Severn obliges, as he knew damn well he would, mustering all the coldness he can in the vagueness of his gesture, and indicates the empty chair, Keats' chair. But he will not say a word. Mrs Pidgeon takes her time, picks off a loose hair she's noticed on her skirt and drops it elaborately onto the boards, briskly rubbing her thumb against her finger.

'I thought it best to leave them to it,' she continues,

161

calm as you like. 'Let them get their sleep where they can. This brisk sea air seems to have improved things for them.'

Does she intend to take an ironic tone with him? He itches to upbraid her, but wipes his hand across his mouth to prevent it. To clarify her intent, Mrs Pidgeon puts the emphasis on certain words for him, as if defining them, once and for all.

'I'd say a good rest is what we all could do with, seeing what we've all been put through.'

At this, Severn draws himself up a little, puts down his sketch-pad with deliberation, folds his arms across his chest; all of this to address her. If she will take issue... It would be so much better, so much cleverer, to say nothing at all, shake his head at her, but it's not in his nature. Shouldn't be in anyone's. Talk's what separates us from the beasts. It's more a matter of how little he can manage to say. His chin jutting out, a Cornwall of defiance, he waits for her to make herself unmistakeable, though his smile disobeys him, and slants off derisively. He feels her justification – if there can be one – coming in a deeper intake of breath, but refuses to look up.

'Mr Severn, since it seems you have nothing to say on this or any matter, may I ask, do you mean to wilfully misrepresent me for the duration of this voyage and make our lives a hundred times more miserable? A gentleman like yourself?'

162

He suspected she'd resort to this; the disreputable swell up unpleasantly with imagination and think nothing of voicing low thoughts.

'And are you saying, sir, in your silence, that you intend to see me in this poor light and no other, for the rest of the voyage? Is this to be it?'

'Madam,' he looks at her as fully as he can, 'it is.'

'And there is to be no let up whatsoever?'

This would have been the moment, at a supper or in someone's garden, to stand up, bow and walk away, but the Atlantic doesn't care for men's evasions, their fulsome displays of pique. Here, the bare, boarded stage is cluttered with coils of sodden, earthy rope; spray blunders up mindlessly on the starboard side like unearned applause; a performance would feel cramped and ridiculous. Besides, he has determined not to quit his position.

'You do realize, Mr Severn, that when I agreed to take up this position, escorting Miss Cotterell across the wide ocean, there was no mention from her dear father – too preoccupied with business to take care of her himself – of what turns out to be a most distressing condition. Oh no. No, there was little talk of that. No mention of the fainting fits, the diarrhoea, the terrible headaches; no mention of what she might cry out when in pain. Nor of the burden she was bound to become. There, indeed, was a sharp game played the day I walked into that house. There I was, trying for a new start, for a way to get away, so I never saw their trap. And yes, the money mattered, of course it did, and they paid me well. So I smiled at all the smiles they'd prepared for me, ate the sugared almonds and marvelled at her, she so sweetly condescending, impossible, it seemed, she'd ever be trouble of any kind.'

Severn studies her, unsure of how much he's willing to believe.

'And as for the storm, well, you know how it was. It could easily have killed us all. Several times, the end seemed about to come. Wasn't that enough to shake your faith in your poor friend too? Weren't you afraid of dying too? Or was that fear solely the preserve of the ladies?

'Mr Severn,' she says, as though his attention had drifted, 'there's one thing I want you to know above all. In difficult times – and there have been many – I've always stood firm. My conduct has been beyond reproach. I've never once given in to sorrow's surfeits. I've grieved, alone, in private, the loss of a husband whose mind had got left behind, somewhere in Spain, defending our country against the menace of Buonaparte. Strangers would never guess at the troubles I had. That was always a matter of pride to me.

'But to die out here at someone else's beck and call, for a girl who bought me with her lies, to find myself wailing and wading in the dark and cold, to be drowned amongst strangers, unheard and unloved,

164

in a sea I scarcely knew the name of before, to the sound of her shrieks and for what? For the sake of my abused good nature, for the chance to escape my brother's beneficence, endlessly waved in my face like a handful of feathers? Did you really expect a lady of my disposition – frank and exacting, as it is – to go out like a saint, like the poor patron saint of nursemaids? Do you expect me to sit here and say sorry for wishing her somewhere else?

Severn clears his throat. There's no chance of the scene going off lightly. Yet even in her outcry, he's sure she's calculating, even now. And he'd rather be spared the detail. What eats at this woman is none of his concern. It's no surprise that her tirade – for that is what it is – has cooled their relations further.

'I'm sure, Mrs Pidgeon, upon our arrival in Naples, that Miss Cotterell's doctor will be notified of all the trouble you've taken and the degree of care you've handed out to her. You have, since you put the case most forcibly, been to great lengths, I see that now. Like the rest of us, you've carried out your duties to the best of your abilities in trying circumstances. I see too that you have not the laws of friendship to fall back on as I have with my dear Keats.'

Mrs Pidgeon can't believe this is all he has to say. She leans forward in her chair, to make herself as clear and as hostile as she can, and smiles, as if pinching out a candle.

'You have a cool way with forgiveness, Mr Severn, which does you little credit.'

Severn hears his own voice struggle to control its pitch.

'Candour at your service madam. Though I will promise you this much. That her brother, when he wonders at the distance between you and your charge, will be fully apprised of the difficulties in which we found ourselves. But to wish, as you did, another dead, one so tender and with so much to hope for, why that is not charity, madam, that is not charity as I have been taught it at all. And for all your grievances, madam, which I shall never – rest assured – under-estimate again, it would behove you to show a little more repentance if you wish your fellow passengers to give you good-day.'

He must have the upper hand, since Mrs Pidgeon's eyes have narrowed during this. He makes as if to rise.

'And who are you to tell me this? You with your eternal high hopes for the girl, you with your romantic notions?'

The two of them are breathing heavily as if having wrestled each other down to the planks. Their red, startled faces register the shock of how open they have been. They're both forced to look away, like lovers who have reached the end, regretting their effusions. Why have they let themselves become like this? As the anger goes out in their eyes, they turn from each other as if

166

released from a humiliating dance. The coarse Atlantic light exposes her meanness, making her appear savage and dirty and dull. Zealous was never in her key; she never felt so out of tune, so oddly tense and unstrung. Another time will have to serve.

Irregular Italian verbs

On a good day, when there's sunshine, he tries learning the rest of them off by heart. He closes his eyes and mouths them to himself.

There are a few he still has trouble with. On purpose, not wanting to appear finished. He has Severn test him.

'Assumed?'

'Assunto.'

'Pretended?'

'Easy. Finto.'

'Tormented?'

'Afflitto.'

'Laughed at?'

'Ah. I always have problems with this one. Something like derido?'

'Nearly. It's deriso.'

'Ah yes. Deriso, deriso.'

'How about extinguished, as in a flame?'

'That's spento.'

The Boarding Party

After the warning-shot is fired, after the commotion on deck and the galley-boy with the fright of his life still fresh in his face running to tell them – 'The Portuguese are coming!' – things grow very tense and quiet.

'What now?' resents Mrs. Pidgeon, folding away a letter she's been re-reading. 'What can anyone want from the likes of us?' Whenever she's put at a disadvantage, the trace of a sneer comes back. 'I thought we'd agreed we only want to be left alone.' The two invalids sit up as best they can. Keats puts his book down. Miss Cotterell's puffy eyes grow wider and wider, forgetting how to blink.

'What are they like, these Portuguese? Are we at war with them? Will they at least be civil to us?'

Severn's attempts to steady them all and to stay calm – a rising high-pitched helplessness – provides the only amusement. Keats was intending to shrug the whole thing off, but, despite himself, his heartbeats clamour, tetchily. He looks around in the dim, watching the air get staler, trying to see the rest of them heaped in their bunks in the same terms the foreigners will: the polite squalor of those forced to be over-familiar. The stubbornness of pestilence. A festering sinfulness. An unmade breeding-ground, brooding quarters. A cabin of ill-repute.

They follow the footsteps up on deck with their eyes, trying to work out which are the Portuguese. The pause after the doors are opened shows only clear blue, teases them. Then a blur of scowling badness steps into the light. The stairs creak accordingly. The villain's worn, buckled shoes and frayed trousers start their descent. A black scabbard bounces jauntily. His tread is scarily purposeful. Mrs. Pidgeon gulps. Miss Cotterell says her silent prayers. Severn peers up, curious to see the knavery of the fellow. Keats is grave-quiet. Their respect is forced, tangible, rises up against their wishes. The lead man is taking forever; has stopped to take advice, sounds less sure of himself.

The short, tubby man in the stained red shirt, who has no scars, nor twitching, lascivious eye, who leans down to take them all in in one sweeping glare, sees more than enough. Suspicion turns to alarm. He screws his necktie up to his nose and motions to his companion to go back up. Nothing here. The few repeated words he mutters sound like a valediction, a verdict, a curse. His leaving creates a blank, guilty disappointment – in what way have they failed him? – before the relief sweeps through them and the blood sneaks back blindly to their hearts.

Afterwards, Severn having scrambled out and taken up a position by the steps, as if on guard, listening to make sure, shaping his defiance now that they've gone, his white face amusingly knitted, the open V of his white shirt billowing heroically, they talk and talk about what might have been. The scrape they were almost

170

in. The rogues bring out the best of spirits in them, a commonality of the reprieved; they feel free now to imagine all kinds of grisly or debonair ends.

'You should have seen yourself Keats,' Severn launches in. 'I never saw such a blaze about you; you could have singed me with one of your looks.'

'Didn't I tell you we should each keep a pistol by our side? A man can never be too careful,' he says, crinkling his eyes. 'Did you see the shock spread through his face when he saw us all down here? I swear there were tears in his eyes. Clearly, we were not what he was looking for. I think, Severn, your natural fierceness saw him off.'

'You saw that too? Though, surely, if his eyes lingered for a moment, it was in Miss Cotterell's direction?' Severn wants to draw her in, she's been so down of late.

'You flatter me, Mr. Severn,' she smiles, gratefully. 'There was no gleam whatsoever in those eyes.'

'The eyes of a brigand,' adds Keats.

'Rather, I'd've thought, the eyes of a brigand in a sea-faring novel. His bristling eyebrows. His scornful pride. Etcetera.'

'Ah, the unmistakeable lure of the high seas.'

'Oh, there's powerful drama in these Portuguese, Mr. Keats.'

'Shame he didn't stay and offer us a song,' says Severn.

'An Iberian lullaby,' says Keats.

'Something heartfelt.' For once, Mrs Pidgeon

171

joins in and receives no admonishing looks. Fear has improved them.

'But in any case, song or no song, there was a fate we would have prevented or died in the trying!'

And so the afternoon wears on in talk that no one will remember and it's not till late, when the boy calls from the galley about who's having what, that Keats leans back on his elbows and suddenly thinks of Fanny – where she's walked today, in whose company, whether his friends have shown her the kindnesses Keats asked them to – and falls foul of himself once again.

The sea sidles up to him, full of itself, swollen and insinuating. It goes on sporting itself, thrashing about like someone who can't settle, sprawling openly in damp, salty sheets, doing its old-fashioned, old harlot's tease. He wrinkles a prim nose at its curdling invitations.

You know what? He can't actually help himself, can he? He knows where she'll be, thinly grieving, sitting in a cooling silence with her mother. The two of them having been abandoned by him, can now be prevailed upon by friends to take some exercise, pass the best part of an evening out every now and then. Because he's not there to watch them, watch over them, he means. He sees, beside the lamp, a dropped novel of the sort he'd rather she wasn't reading. No matter if she's tired of it; that's not the one he'd have chosen. He sees normality – ever so friendly and banal – beginning to win out, stealing up on her, urging her to take good heart. When she should be worrying herself threadbare. She pulls the red curtains against the coming evening. That's right, Fanny. There are wolves in Hampstead, packs of salivating snarlers, lip-lickers; flirtatious near-neighbours calling with their generous condolences, honey-words at every turn. Men at large.

From here, nodding knowledgeably, pointless in an ocean, he can see through it all, society: the idle, fireside plans on damp afternoons; some new gentleman come

173

to pay his respects, pawing and doffing, come to hone their whimsical skills. The type who can play decorum's game. Someone who, quite by chance, might call by in foul weather, drenched and affable, the state of his boots a cause for consternation, requiring all her attention. Would she, deaf to her promises, put down her handiwork, glad of the distraction? She could be ambushed by a coterie, invited more than once to a quadrille, where, left in a corner, looking unguarded and vulnerable – worse, worse, available! – she might offer her hand to some viper's show of elegance.

Thinking of her like this, like prey, is all he allows himself, but even thinking is inconstant. And though it does him continual, conspicuous harm, he wants this picture he has of her, staring at the curtains, completely at a loss over how to live her life, to burn right through him. Only when he can imagine her breaking down, tearing at the pins in her hair, blaming him in that childish way of hers, will he be satisfied. She's hurting; her mother will go to her. It's then he triumphs, pretending he can hold her to him once again, as if, guarding the candle flame, he were to take intrepid steps down a draughty passage.

Though it's really the sea that's to blame. It has no place to settle down and call its own.

The same things

Its one trick never fails to impress. From the depths of its black sleeves, the magus-sea flourishes endless whitecaps which hiss and snivel for a while before expiring with a sigh. The currents are impossible to detect, however hard you watch for them. Lumpy, uncultivated fields of nonplussed grey-green in every direction. Sometimes, as if to break the dreary spell, a couple of snarling waves collide then stand back from each other, as if affronted.

'Old Misprision's been gone a while, Severn.'

'She must have her eye on the watch.'

'What's he done to offend her? Not watching closely enough?' Severn goes to find out what's keeping her, from a safe distance. That leaves the two of them, talking, either side of the curtain.

'What is it you miss, more than anything, about England?' she asks.

'What I'd give now to see a grassy rise, with a row of ordinary fence-posts striding down, at an angle, to meet it halfway, knowing that, over the brow, lay the suburbs, some market gardens, smoke rising, the spires of London a morning's walk away.'

'What else?'

'In the stand of trees, September time, have you ever noticed the first to take up the taint of autumn, the wind-picked one? Or in June, how the new sycamore

175

seeds, conjoined in perfect symmetry, blush red for a week, as if the whole tree were suddenly in love?'

'In our garden, there are two silver birches, spindly and nervous, which stand out pale against the hedgerow.'

'Or what about brown linseed fields, prickle-brittle, in early October, very drab and yet comfortingly familiar? Coming across cart-ruts in fresh snow, no way of knowing which direction whoever it was was going?'

'I used to love the snow. Oh isn't it wonderful, how we miss the very same things!'

'We could still be there now,' Keats reminds her.

'And I still don't know why I'm not.'

A long silence.

'Have you forgiven yourself yet?'

'Have you?'

Keats shrugs. They smile at each other. She has one more question.

'Can they imagine us, those still at home, do you think?'

'I hope for their sakes they can't.'

Becalmed

By degrees the wind has died. The sea, slow to respond, swarthier now, sulks in a gelid pique. The level, stilled waters seem eerier than ever. The coastline flirts with them, sea-haze shrouding something purportedly Spain. Distant, listless, the sun bores through nuisance-cloud, only to give in, still dazed and spectral, to persistent, churlish fogs. Mrs Pidgeon, undaunted, climbing to the poop deck, vanishes in and out of them. Hidden in the midst of a strange hush, she keeps as still as she can, feeling momentarily reprieved. When she comes back down, she blinks the droplets out of her lashes, reports on the little she's seen. No one shows much interest. Passions don't seem worth the rousing here. It's no longer just Miss Cotterell who seems drowsy, abashed; they all seem more remote from each other, as though dumbstruck by the differences which have opened up between them: those still good, those going to the bad. The unsparing wind had made them restless, had loosened their tongues, setting things free. Now, as the mornings slowly come clear, they seem, disconcertingly, like strangers to be endured once again, self-conscious and distrustful, mewling to themselves behind their bars, licking swollen paws.

Later, from her accustomed chair on deck, in weak sunlight, Mrs Pidgeon scrutinises them. One by one, she has repealed them all; as far as she's concerned, that's

177

very much that for the days ahead. She can't wait for the voyage to end; she sighs and crosses her ankles again. Her white, scrubbed hands take up their embroidery: now, where was she? She hasn't been able to concentrate properly since her talk with Mr. Severn. Her needle flashes. *She's* not the one at fault. Her constant diligence-vigilance goes on. It's the others that have lied to *her*. *She's* the one that's been misled, make no mistake. How could she have guessed the girl would deteriorate like that, lying down for hours at a time, for all the world like she were dead?

Miss Cotterell had better last till Naples. She wouldn't want anything complicating her conscience. Explaining Miss Cotterell's decline to her brother – he who can do no wrong – was going to be problematic enough. She hates a lie. Especially one badly told. Perhaps she's just too scrupulous.

Old Misprision's heart is in a parlous state, sore and getting sorer, sourer. *Tut tut tut*, it goes, adding a disparaging beat. When she coughs, because they've all got something wrong with them now, haven't they, she wheezes up bitterness, a phlegmy, chalky cliff-face of a thing. It makes the others look at her and frown. But why's it only the rich and the sick who are allowed to complain?

From now on, she expects the days to go by just the same. Watching the invalids weaken and avoid her, hearing the young men's clatter, thinking they're clever,

178

hearing them tire, run out of funny. Like watching an overloaded cart spilling hay down the lane, the odd wisps, first of all, and then huge ungainly clumps, till there's next to nothing left. No doubt her presence will be tolerated, her views noted, her company eked out between them. At least, that's what she supposes.

She pinches the fold of loose skin under her jaw, rubs where her necklace has been. The others look stumped in their chairs. Mr Severn can't think what to say. Miss Cotterell has her eyes closed, as usual. Mr Keats is in a towering gloom. She has her secrets, too. At night, for example, she treats herself to the dream of her warm lieutenant, she inhales the unbuttoned might-have-been: dozing in his arms, sinking into him, amazed at where a bit of old-fashioned cheek and a good long look have led her to, that uniform of his brightly straddling the back of a chair. She snuggles back down with him...

The things she's kept to herself! Not like poor Miss Cotterell, always wanting to confide. Time was when she knew a thing or two about innocence, about the charm of hopes deferred. Skipping down Ludgate Hill, being minded to be silly, running ahead of her parents, without a bonnet, to catch her breath at the bottom, full of the beat of the blood gone to her head, ringing in her ears; Sunday afternoons spent down by the river, alone, lying in tall, tousled grasses, thinking of boys; fidgeting in the family pew and ignoring her mother's hisses, enduring her stony looks afterwards; hearing her father come in through the dark, back from the ale-house, long after she was supposed to be asleep, hearing him blowing hard to keep from falling over, picturing the long arc of his piss splashing in and over the rim of the pot.

Night air

Not something *else* she's not supposed to! Having woken to no distress – patting herself in disbelief – and having dressed in haste, she can't wait to feel its warmth swirl up soft and sure about her. She fiddles with the last of her buttons, impatiently. Should make for excellent brooding up there. Or marvelling. The stars, she's been told, will look further out than ever above a warmer sea.

The mainsail rises up, as if drawn to its full height by the moon, stretched way above what she thought possible. Like this, washed in spectral light, it seems both flattered and flattened, a dream-material without any unsightly seams and cicatrices of stitches. The enormous white yards of cloth ripple to a suggestion from the south-west, puff and snap like Lady Putupon awaiting her carriage to the ball. Beyond them, the firmament blazes, its virulence displayed like a brilliant, alarming rash. There they are. What have they got to tell her, apart from their loneliness, their beauty? Pricks of conscience. Flickering bewitchery. If only they could sing. But it would be a sustained high note pitched beyond our hearing.

Of course, they're much more useful out here than they are on land. She doesn't know them half as well as she should. Anonymous fires always on the brink of expiring. Can they all have names? And can anyone name them what they like? Can an eighteen-year-old

181

design the skies, as well as any other? Isn't there still time?

The night-sky vaunts itself in a sheer she can't take in, craning back. She reels a little, trying to adjust, perceiving that they waver up there, in shifting, relative distances; they appear to grow more and more unsteady. The black spires of the main and mizzen mastheads point out new surprises, clusters, densities, intensities, patterns of sugary dustings and straggling peppery fires. It's like a scandal up there; as if everyone's come out to whisper, contribute, steal a look for themselves. The scattered streaks of stardust must be the result of some calamity, at the furthest reach of God. She wonders, can stars ever be set free?

'You all right, Miss?'

In her surprise, she places her hand on her heart. It's just the watch's voice.

'Hadn't someone best take you back down?'

How it irks her not to be alone. She says nothing, for fear her throat might give her emotion away. Caught out, she covers the fires in her eyes with the heels of her hands, extinguishes what matters in herself, before turning round. She can't make the man out correctly; she can still see the afterglow of the stars, reddening, each time she blinks.

'Are you sure you – shouldn't you be below?'

'I am quite well, quite well,' she assures him. 'Thank you for your concern. I was just admiring the night.

There are no rules against that, I take it? I shall make my own way down in good time.'

'Right you are, Miss. Just looking out for you, that's all.'

But the sky has been spoiled for her. The glitter seems showy and brazen now. She shivers in her coat. Men. First they neglect her, then they cosset her. No matter, she will take one last turn.

What had Mr Keats said?

'Keep your eyes open. They say the end of the world is out here somewhere. Before you know it, you're swept out in an immense waterfall, poured into oblivion like a leaf from the pot.'

He was only teasing. But there's a dream she keeps on having, not dissimilar to this, from which she wakes up drenched and thirsting, though strangely happier. Ever since that first coughing fit on the stairs, back from the theatre, a little enervated, it's true, *but that was all*, she feels she's been skirting the edge of the world.

How much further is it? How will she recognise it when she's finally there? Which country are they going by now?

She walks up and down like a ghost, a pained ghost who knows it can't frighten or haunt, doomed to walk ever thus. Above her, the stars go on being shameless, conducting their lovemaking in all the dark places.

The gift

To her great joy, Miss Cotterell finds herself alone once more with Mr Keats. It could be the last time. Naples can only be days away, the right winds permitting. A flush spreads through her, paramount, like a passionate prayer. For what she is about to do...

Though he must be dozing, since he's been so quiet, she knows by now that the two-inch gap that sometimes appears between the slack in the curtains means he can spy her well enough through the slats of his bunk. If she can get his attention. To begin with, she hums a well-known tune to give herself courage. At all costs she must remain as unselfconscious as possible, act normal, beyond reproach. She'd hate for anyone to think...

What she is about to offer him is consolation. Kindness laid bare. She undresses as if in an inviolate dream, a private space, like a wasted, white Diana inviting trespassers to her pool. She turns unsteadily, rustily, feeling a blush might betray her. She knows not to look up: *that* modesty forbids. To take her mind off what she's up to, she scratches at a spot beneath her shoulder-blades till it must have reddened dramatically. So far, all quite natural. She rolls down her stocking-tops hastily, gauchely, stifling an actress' yawn. Knock-kneed, skinny and timid as a fawn, she steps regretfully out of the hush of her black dress – its puffed sleeves seeming more incongruous with each passing day

184

– blinking rapidly as if emerging from the dark. She imagines herself a woman now; her necklace shows her white throat to advantage.

She turns around irrevocably for him, trembling and marbling in the chill, her chin held high. Her humming has stopped. Heavy footsteps above them come to a halt, as if someone up there had suspected. What must he think? She tries to interpret his silence, the rhythms in his breathing. For as long as she dares, she holds this position, balancing more and more awkwardly, beginning to rock on her heels. It's a shame she's so taut, so thin; she knows her knees and elbows are raw, her thighs are more scrawny than graceful; her once-sweet breasts meagre and sallow. If she can never know the warmth of love, a man's hands pressing the skin of her upper arms as he bends to her with every intention, then this chaste display, her flesh goose-pimpling, will have to do. Let one starved man feast his eyes on her. Sometimes, admiring glances are better supposed than seen. And to think men dream over and over for glimpses of this; or pay for its brief possession; or save themselves like the Bible says and marry with the one thing weighing on their minds.

She can't sustain it; she keeps hearing too many things; every creak's a potential interruption. Her courage finally goes in a twitch of the curtain. Her forearms reach up instinctively, guiltily, to protect her, as if she were hugging nothing but her shame. Words

185

must flutter from her, but she can't think what she's said, as she retrieves her underclothes and begins to step back in to what she was, wondering if that will be possible now, binding herself angrily up once more into all her stupid layers.

Keats, consumed with that strange, resentful thing he has against women, can do nothing with the tears welling and stinging for several minutes, swallows down his silent grieving.

PART FIVE

The Land

Naples, Late October 1820

Hailing distance

In this way, they make their joyous return to the world...

A solitary fishing smack, rocking gently, its one sail furled, is the first proof they're finally there. A swarthy, heavy-set man, quite unremarkable, sits aft, scratching at his head and yawning. Conscious of, but indifferent to, their overhauling shadow, he looks as bored and slovenly as any frontier guard. To them, of course, he's nothing less than simplicity under the sun, the tantalising South's best ambassador, fellowed in deep feeling, an emissary from somewhere they'd almost forgotten existed. His brief, bland look up at them seems somehow honest, warm; all the welcome they could have wished for. No matter that his open-

187

necked shirt looks grubby and worn. No matter that he merely nods and goes about his black-bearded business, inspecting his lines, like his saturnine father and grandfather before him, the knowledge ingrained in the hard, knotted wood of his face. Doesn't he stand for all that's instinctive, spontaneous, Italy's natural bonhomie? They all gawp at him, as if at a phrenologist's case study, longing to recognise the type, like some kind of prized primitive. After a moment, he straightens up, as if struck by a sudden thought, and spits far out into the sea. His barked laugh barely carries to them.

And as they sail on, stunned, submitting, the sun is soon high enough to make them shade their eyes, in a row of uneven salutes. The light extols everything. By now, Keats has regained what composure he can, is determined to see Naples in. He has assured everyone he is much, much better, though he looks wild enough, dishevelled, like a clumsy woodcut of a shipwrecked man.

'You know what I'm thinking?' he says to Severn. 'Somewhere out there, so Virgil would have us believe, is the way to the underworld.'

Severn rests his hand on Keats' shoulder. 'What did I say to you about saying things like that? I won't stand for it, I tell you. And before you think of anything else, take a look at that sky. Have you ever seen colour like it?'

'What, you mean, the blue? Severn, I think I've seen enough. I think I am blued fairly through and through.'

188

'Why do this do to yourself? Why don't you just look at the bay?'

For the sake of his friend, Keats agrees to, for a while. Admittedly, the curve is sublime, offering up its wealth of consolations, its display-case of jeweller's refinements. Gradually, more details emerge, new species. More cliffs assert themselves in a wide, white glare last seen off Yarmouth, Isle of Wight. There's a glimpse of stunted olives; rows of reddening vines; the dark, set teardrops of solitary cypresses. A hint of fragrance curls their way, leading them to stare at a stand of pines which bristles over a cliff-top, stopping abruptly as if aghast at the precipice, stricken roots dangling, their trunks towering high, as if grown tall out of vertigo. Smoke rises from the occasional white-washed cottage, its red-tiled roof ablaze against the blue. People are at home here, getting ready for their work in the fields, in the forest, in the port, reminding each other of what they must face today, bent over a simple, shared breakfast of bread and cheese.

As the coast grows clear, the crew are more than willing to lend a hand. Thank God, they seem to be thinking, our time here is done. They busy themselves back into the habit of happiness, sprucing up the deck, knowing that work with the end in sight is the best kind of work, smacking their lips at the thought of the liquor to be had, all the spices they can choose from. They can feel a sweet soothe coming. An ache in the teeth

189

reminds them of what's on offer. Sure enough, they break out the old tunes, start swigging back the light. They joke with each other, trading familiar insults. It's as if they've remembered their lines, their parts, what knavish jacks they are.

Finally, spread out before them, as they round the last cape, is a grand convergence of boats, as if Naples had sent out a flotilla, anxious to court them, to make amends, there are so many vessels tacking and running and going hard about, their wakes criss-crossing in sport. Severn, for one, feels as though he's being greeted like Nelson himself. See, heroes *do* come back. They cross their first boat leaving port, cutting a remarkable dash, the passengers tanned and robust, smiling over at them, looking eager, relaxed. Keats turns to watch them go. Severn does his waving for him. The strangers wave vigorously back. There are, all in all, so many pleasures to be had. It's been easy to forget that. Most people want to be forgiving and helpful and kind. There could be many more mornings like this...

All around them, on the surface, jauntiness abounds; relief that all those who set out are back safe again. It's a scene ages-old; it could almost be Agamemnon inspecting the review: they pass by gaily-painted fishing-boats, heading further out; an occasional low-slung sloop; pleasure craft, going at a fair rate wherever they please; sturdier, sterner wherries and brigs, laden, earnest, determined not to be outdone.

190

In short, a community of vessels plying and riding the waves, jostling for position, taking up or paying out sails of every description. Like parti-coloured ribbons on a maypole, they ripple out in all directions. A convivial spirit reigns. For a moment, it looks like a floating market-place has set out its stalls. Anything can be purchased here, all the fineries of the world. A Mediterranean harvest-festival. The sea itself might as well be brimming o'er. Miss Cotterell exclaims for all she's worth, pointing out novelties and surprises. Men with unheard-of wares pole in and out of the largest boats, scraping against hulls, delighted to see them, happy for their custom. They reach over baskets of fresh, ripe fruit. Nectarines and figs, oranges, red grapes and melons, more...

* * * *

When the harbourmaster comes alongside, gleaming with self-importance, he leans his flushed, fat face as far out as he can, his eyes popping as he strains to make himself heard. They assume he's delighted to see them. He gesticulates with some urgency. Gusts of excitable vowels blow over them, as if the wind loved only consonants, and greedily whirled them away. What they are left with are snatches of incomprehensible passion. Just what the guidebooks said they'd hear. Severn remarks that whatever the man's saying seems to be

191

causing him considerable pain. The distended balloon of his face is about to burst. His lips stretch and purse, stretch and purse as if limbering up for a leap across an abyss. What's amusing is that not one of them can make out the least of what he wants. For all they know, he could be singing. Arias, of course. From something a little tragic, by the sound of them. He certainly seems very flappable, as if acting in everybody's best interests, looking increasingly likely to take things into his own hands. Which can't for a second keep still. He seems almost desperate. Something is obviously the matter with him – but what? Persistent to the point of absurdity, the man stabs his finger repeatedly at Keats. The others all look at him, as if they'd found the accused, after all, amongst them.

'It can't be me,' says Keats. 'I haven't done anything.'

The shouting match that follows, full of consternation, misapprehensions, frowns and shrugs, in a language mostly lost to the wind, made up of fragments flung across an enormous, unstable divide, syllables that insist on shifting, slipping above the churning depths, a roar of instructions, words without ornament, stripped of subtlety or shade, occupies Keats strangely. Isn't this just the way it's always been? Two people perched high above a treacherous, furtive current, trying to reach out to each other, get their message across. Do souls in heaven have to shout like this, he wonders? He must ask Miss Cotterell this very question.

192

The bad news

They've not seen the captain like this before, not anything like; he was not raised to this pitch by any of the storms. He gives the skies something to think about with a look of due reproach, then proceeds to kick out at pieces of wood, and grind the heels of his hands together. Chafing, he grabs onto a rope and twists till it hurts, preferring the easier pain. The crew shrink away. When he's finished, he catches sight of Severn's question and steadies himself.

'Believe me, I told him. I said not one of us had shown the least sign of it, but he – well, you saw for yourself. Show his kind a rulebook and he'll make them his dying words.'

Severn grimaces sympathetically, and shrugs, still with no idea of what's happened. The captain relents enough to explain.

'Ten days more. That's all of us, without exception. Ten more days aboard ship. No one may go ashore; there is to be no contact with anybody else. Any provisions will be sent up to us. There's been an outbreak of typhus in London, around the time we left. Orders of the king.'

He goes off to give orders of a very different kind. Severn is left looking like he can't take his medicine. Miss Cotterell bites her lip, says something ever so faint and grave, like 'I see.' She looks and looks again at where the captain stood. She's not very clear about what her face is doing, but whatever it is, she can't control it.

'But what about my brother?' she cries out. 'How's he supposed to find me now?' Immediately she wishes she hadn't, then repairs below, unable to contain herself.

'It can't be right,' murmurs Mrs Pidgeon, sitting down. 'It can't be.'

It starts to sink in.

'No, you're right. It isn't,' Keats echoes, finally.

'One of us should go after her,' says Severn automatically, but none of them has any such intention. None of them is even prepared to show willing.

'Ten more days? Ten? Of this? How could they?'

Keats is beginning to understand. The cycle is beginning all over again. Outbreaks. Restrictions. Punishments. But it's the frigger's disease that he's got, not typhus.

'Typhus? Typhus?'

He shouts the filthy, futile word out as though it were a heresy. Severn won't meet his eye.

'In which of God's ways can this be considered fair?'

Silence. No one answers his challenge. He stoops, struggling for more air, and comes to a stop. He sits down heavily next to Severn. They are all turned to stone.

'Well,' sighs Mrs Pidgeon, eventually. 'That didn't take long. Now that we're back amongst the world.' She looks up to see if anyone has heard her, but no one cares what she says or thinks.

194

Muted, servile, they are shepherded to their mooring-place. The crew look shrunken, galled, staring thirstily at the shore, at what they can't have in abundance there. Other crews watch them taking the news badly. The *Maria Crowther* herself is nothing if not obedient. She doesn't understand either. She lies, where she is told, under the shadow of the great sandstone fortress. How appropriate, Keats thinks. Its solid bulk oppresses him, prevents any chance of them seeing the rest of the bay. Who'd have thought it possible: from the Tower of London to another great prison bricking him in. Props of ailing monarchies, symbols of a sick, intolerant world. He imagines the poor devils lowered into black water that comes up to their throats. All the instruments in the service of the lords. God only knows the specializations that have gone on in there. And out here, only the mind, once again, is at liberty. They are all of them condemned, like bad meat; as if the wrong smell – the English smell, the smell of the outlaw, the radical – comes off them.

The port, now Severn looks about him, knowing the truth of it, does seem unnaturally cluttered. Hundreds of ships ride at anchor in the roads. They, too, look ill-at-ease, down-on-their-luck. They have the sorrowful air of slaves, marked out for sale, shackled in incommunicable misery, far from home, awaiting further orders, new owners.

'Naples,' he explains to the ladies, when they are ready to bear with a story, when a kind of dissolute disappointment has settled about their hearts, a slackening off from the first great injustice, 'was founded by adventurous Greeks. Long before Rome had been dreamt of, they came upon this. Imagine their delight. Discovering this, they must have felt much the same force of wonder as we all did this morning, though they must have been far more afraid. They would have known the bay was too perfect to be given up lightly by those already here. They would have seen the hearth-fires from their ships, must have seen the land was already settled. Who'd give up beauty like this without...'

Keats would love to talk them all round. Get through this, as everything else, with a string of words. Flat on his back, eyes swollen and closed, he talks himself hoarse into the candle-light, a tour-guide taking them back to normality, its familiar streets, its notable ruins, unsure if the two women are actually listening. They sound as if they are. He speaks from memory, coughing every now and again, as if dusting off a dream. He knows more than he thought possible; most of which was never much use before. Triremes. Sparta. The Parthenon. None of these ever kept creditors from his door.

Afterwards, when the others are all obviously asleep, his voice become a whisper, he strokes his throat, feeling for where it's most tender. Why can't someone who knows so much of these things, who could dredge up and name half the dead from the Styx, why can't he make his own private Helicon to believe in? Think of a dream pasture leading to a stream, where, rooting about down by the reed-beds, he might chance upon his own reflection – his pale eyes undimmed, his shepherd-boy locks tousled by the ripples. That would be worth stumbling across, a find as good as a clearing; imagine what encounters, what bathing could be had there... Always a thrill in the air, some likelihood coming; the sound of the chase; hooves drumming the earth; sinuous harp and flute music; a young woman stooping to add to her basket of fruit; a whisper in the myrtle leaves. All of this south-facing, in an eternal Spring, where all manner of trees can be blossom-heavy at once, where shadows are kind, where dews go on pearling day-long. Then to replenish it with lovable, talkative gods and sprites that get on well; to hint at distant hills of olive groves and meadows rich with meadowsweet, bell-flowers.

He could create sun enough there to persuade himself under the dapples, a grassy bank made for his shape amongst scattered stones and columns. Light like that would tarry awhile, long enough for him to have the animals talk, having first transformed them to his own devices. Then he'd sit and hear tell of mulish magic and foxy devotion; listen to tales of a snake's self-reliance or an owl's daft scrapes.

197

Once, he could easily imagine like that, write for hours in a white steady light, the heat of his vision flushing his cheeks. Lines came to him, unsought. Words would come to nuzzle against him, like so many shy creatures. He used to lie alone, swishing at flies, seizing his opportunities, in a Hampstead back-garden's-worth of Olympia. So why can't he stay there in the grove for longer? What was all that learning for, if he can't surround himself with it now?

But now, when the faint music stops, and the haze lifts tenderly, who's that he sees silhouetted against the light? It could be almost anyone from his old circle. Someone he knows but can't for the life of him place. Someone disturbing his peace, trying hard to tell him something. The first yellow leaf curls down. Could it be his old friend Charles Cowden Clarke beckoning him over, or generous Hunt, or brilliant, flustered Reynolds, spouting Law, or even, God forbid, Georgiana, his delectable sister-in-law, her shoulders freckled like a late gold pear, trailing her hand in the water's silks, suggesting there's a new world they should visit where yet lovelier women lie in wait, willing to call his name?

198

His poor, pusillanimous soul. Keats fixes on it, curled up on itself at the bottom of his bunk, whimpering like a disconsolate dog. A bad dog. A dog with mange.

His skin's the same colour as a whore's exhausted taupe. When he reaches up to feel his cheek, it scrapes his fingers, as rough as stale bread. This is what he's dwindled to, under the sheets, a stripped and whittled stick not worth playing with.

Severn's seen him, looking at nothing, like the sad stone lion in the British Museum, Assyrian, its fierceness effaced, all its colouring gone. Only the black eye-pits remain, from where the precious stones were stolen.

He has more dreams he could do without. A dream of the blind, black leech distending, distending, then crawling up along him, with something to say in his ear. A dream of saltwater in which he thrashes with a lunatic's energy, then gives up blessedly, overwhelmed.

He wakes up to the dry gasp of his sweating self, a wheezy sag of prickling skin and a heart that's overcompensating. His loves are out of focus. From far away, reassurances gather like lean and knowing birds of prey, birds with glittering beaks, and dead eyes. He can't afford to listen.

He might as well be a backward child, left outside in a downpour, twisting his hair to the roots, gurgling, unable to make himself plain.

Inevitability's dry mouth. A tongue like clay. Blister lips. His temples palpate, his skull-plates tremble with the effort – the head's final tectonics.

As for his lungs, his lungs resemble Venice, exquisite, intricate and doomed, sinking in their tarry, tubercular lagoon. A winter tree inverted, poisoned by a sticky mistletoe.

He is leaking, listing, rusting. Roof-timbers split lengthways, his scalp roars; a whisper sounds like a bell's clapper. This is the final tolling, the tolling he knows full well.

But no, he mustn't die, not yet, Severn said, though this, so they say, is all Naples is good for.

On easeful death

Still no sign of Charles. That's a whole day now. She has reined herself in so hard for so long, now that she's given in, she stumbles into her bunk, panting, head lowered, heavy-legged, like a tow-path shire-horse glimpsing its final pasture. She sinks down, minnowing her hips under the sheet, determined not to get up till he appears. Let him see her like this; let him see what she's been through.

She hasn't the strength for anything anymore. All afternoon, she slips in and out of consciousness. Each time she wakes, and senses he's not there, it's like another twist of a tourniquet, bringing colour to her cheeks, but at a dreadful cost. Sometimes, she wakes to a terrible thirst, thrashing at the sheets in alarm, as if having dreamed an attacker, and makes the same dry crackles that kindling makes when it catches. Mrs Pidgeon holds out a glass for her. She drinks, making those clucks that gulping children make, then drinks again. While she's recovering, she blinks her thanks, her eyes still wide and frightened, huge over the rim of the glass.

Hours pass without her daring to say a word. Needless to say anything. Every 'h' scorches the back of her throat. Waiting like this, for her brother to come, requires so little of her, that when they bring her a little clear soup, she makes no fuss at all, sits up against the pillow quietly with her hands trembling on the covers.

201

The original skin-and-bone.

She's tried to look within, but there's not enough there. The Lord's reach fumbles. She devotes herself instead to her idea of her brother, even now being rowed out in haste to greet her. No one has told her why her voice is going, that she shouts out the mangled ends of childhood prayers – *till earth is in heaven* – when she's delirious.

The captain is worried what this might mean, if she can't last it out. One by one, they come down to look at her, and worry still more. Even Keats. He motions to Mrs Pidgeon to leave her side. It will do him good to have someone to watch over. He has a book for company. He promises he will sit tight, be careful not to disturb her. When the volume he's holding slips to the floor, she stirs, sees it's him.

'No, not yet. But he'll get here soon. They sent word immediately.'

Her dangerous lips move. He must be careful not to lean too far over her to hear her.

'Why keep anything from me now?' she whispers. Keats, surprised at her suspicion, draws back, swears he's said true. Why should he of all people keep anything from her? Her symptoms are less than a month in advance of his. They should, really, be ashamed of their reticence. They have perhaps a few minutes together. Once Charles arrives, he'll not be parted from her. Thereafter she'll be cared for at great

202

expense. Somewhere ashore the servants and nurses are already gathering. Let them share one more look at what might have been, whisper together, like plotters hearing footsteps coming, knowing they're about to be caught, hauled out into the light.

She wets her lips and thinks of a beginning.

'Has the time not yet come when we feel that none of this,' – she indicates her suffering – 'matters anymore?'

'No. No, I don't think so. I don't think that time ever comes. I think we just go on feeling.'

'On and on?'

'That's what I'm afraid of, yes.'

'But when it comes round to our turn?' she asks, more fervently.

'Our turn?'

'To see what heaven has in store.' She nods, as if to encourage him.

'Yes, well, heaven will be well-stocked, as I'm sure...'

'But how will we get there, when it's time?'

'As for that, that I have planned. I intend to go out in as little pain as possible. I am of course hoping to be well-received.' She smiles at this. He's succeeding. 'Besides, you'll soon have your brother here, seeing to your every need. And then there'll be no need for the rest of us.'

'And you'll have...?'

'Yes.'

'There's no easy way of getting there then?'

203

'I don't predict angels myself. Not that I'm saying for one moment others don't deserve them.'

'But beforehand, is it possible to feel the actual...' She waits for Keats to finish this for her.

'That's for the doctors. Their little secret.'

'But didn't you say... At your time in the hospital you must have seen...'

'Things I'd rather I hadn't, oh yes... But that was long ago and had more to do with the way the surgeons worked.'

'But how do people allow it to happen, to let themselves go, not knowing?'

'Ah that. Well, as for that...' Keats spreads his hands.

Oh, Charles!

The gloved hands are the first thing Severn sees, the grasp of the man. He hauls himself over without help and lands a little unfortunately, stumbling a pace or two before he can gather himself, as if carried forward not by momentum, but by his own resolve. *Ah well*, thinks Severn, *at least he exists!*

He has the look of the relieving soldier who scales the walls, only to find himself too wearied to take in what the long siege has done to the city below. His eyes roll in the effort to find their focus, looking everywhere for her, for that embrace. The rescuer, primed with inordinate fears, doesn't know quite where to rescue yet. He reels across the deck, flushed and uncertain, wheeling round for answers. Yes, he wears the wealthy man's clothes, carries them with a financier's dash – virtue made spry – but he has that hunted look of those who, forced to wait for the ones they love, remain painfully short of news: he looks as if he has come prepared to be appalled. The *Maria Crowther* should have come in about two weeks ago. He must have been living on his nerves ever since.

Trellissed by the rigging's shadow, as if woven into an unchanging pattern of mourning, Severn lets go of the back of Keats' chair and steps out to console him:

'You must be Charles, Charles Cotterell?'

'My sister? She's still with you?'

Charles' handshake has all the grip Severn expected,

205

that fortitude he's heard so much about. He can't help thinking of all the currency that has gone through those sleek fingers, as he clasps the man's arm. Charles breaks free at once; he can have no sense of what it means for Severn to hold onto someone as solid as this, so healthy and valued and real, come straight from the world they've been denied all access to. For isn't Severn, too, in his own way, in need of rescue, longing for another's reassurances? Charles' impatience, his shrugging himself free from conventions, is a disappointment, albeit emphatically natural – he has a banker's forthrightness in all his movements. He takes Severn by the shoulders, to stop him before he protests.

'Yes, I know. Thank God I'm here. But there's no time for all that. Where is she?'

Severn stammers, taken completely by surprise, and manages to indicate below. Just in time, he calls out to Charles' disappearing purposeful back,

'She's not at all well, you know...'

'We'll talk some more,' he shouts out, then ducks inside.

'Well,' says Severn to a smiling Keats still getting to his feet, 'we'll still be here, waiting. We're not allowed anywhere else.'

'Not with all our faults.'

'Our taints.'

* * * *

206

When he comes back out, Severn and Keats have moved their chairs to stay facing the sun and watch him walk over. Keats shuts his volume of Richardson's *Clarissa*, stops thinking about the letters he can't bring himself to send. Severn gets up on his behalf. Both of them are looking out for a sign of what Charles has been through – a pronounced stoop; regret about the chin; the furrows in his brow should be cross-hatched like a Rembrandt etching. But no. Same gait, same impatience. That decisiveness must be inherent. Not even a blurring of his composure. He opens his mouth, ready to tell them how much he is in their debt, and nothing comes out. He tries again. Keats and Severn stare, urging him on. Nothing. He puts his hand up to his cheek, as if feeling for a wound.

'I didn't know,' he says. 'I didn't know what to say to her.'

How he is

When the night comes in, more suddenly than they'd prepared themselves for, the singing begins. Only then, as if the dark confers the necessary confidence or sorrow, does a single voice strain out from one of the boats around them. Usually unaccompanied, but sometimes to a pipe or fiddle or drum, it carries across the still water and they listen to the songs men sing when they're far from home.

Charles has decided to stay, much to Mrs Pidgeon's consternation. He has taken the bunk above his sister's, but gets dressed and undressed on the men's side of the curtain. A cold rain has caught up with them, forcing them below. The men swap life stories. Charles is most diverting; he knows a great deal, has travelled extensively and, in his time, has seen plenty. He talks with pride of Naples, promises them trips out of town. Most certainly, he will show them where the Hamiltons lived; if they like, take them to the lip of the volcano. In return, without meaning to, they fill him with longing for England. Severn does most of the describing. His hands are happy now, gesturing high and low. Keats hears them murmuring, laughing, exclaiming. As usual, he has no intention of saying what he's thinking...

If they'd have let him stay, yes, *if they'd only have let him stay like he wanted,* he'd have quietened in due course, settling to go, surrounded by the things he loved. October's frosts and fogs would visit the garden, shrouding and stiffening the earth, snouts against the windows, peering in at his deterioration. Better than this – this – suffocation, forever cramped and champing. Better than all these delays on the way to – where? To somewhere else unknown, unknowable and probably not worth knowing, sorties into the inhospitable.

How is he now? Severn keeps asking, when it should be what is he now? Why is he now? He answers with the pained smiles of silence, instead of this: like a very ancient Greek, figured in red and black on that urn of his, sunk in inescapable sorrow, one paint-flaked hand upraised, knowing this is not the chase, not the sacrifice, not the procession. That's how he is.

Happy returns

Finally, they have their permission, but by the time the order comes through, Miss Cotterell is so franked with distress, so fevered, so low, she can't make much sense of her return, can't really tell what's world any more. Brought out into the open for the first time in days, she hears her breathing intensify, as if something were frightening her, but she can't see what. The sky seems to drop its vastness down several flights at once, its blue scream widening, its colossal weight bearing down wickedly on her. She flinches. Someone shouts, 'Don't look up yet!' and fumbles at her, his thick, curled fingers pressed immediately onto her eyes. She can hear someone hiss in a language that must mean her harm. She knows she's in some kind of trouble. When she looks up to see what kind, there are shadows on all the strange faces in front of her.

Behind them, caught in full sun, a brilliant city surrounded by hills goes on and on in all directions, steepling and spilling away, unscalable, incomprehensible, purposely glittering at her. Why are they thinking of taking her there? In all those streets, they will surely lose her. Where are the lemon groves? The orange-scented breezes? All she can smell is the reek of the dock: fish skin, fish bones, fish heads. She feels herself starting to gulp at the air, which all at once seems to dart at her, snipe at her, snatching her breath. Why would it do this? She feels that for this to be happening, she must have done a great deal of wrong – but what? She throws her head backward, as if stricken, makes one of her hands fend it away, shooing at the brightness, the unfairness, waving it down, like a leaping dog that's got no owner. Goodbye.

'Charles!' she calls out, without warning. 'Charles! Goodbye, goodbye!'

Then someone she knows well is sitting beside her, rubbing the backs of her hands. She remembers now. All that hurt and concern. So, she has yet to recover. If it isn't a doctor – and it can't be – it must be her brother. Charles has found her somewhere nice. Charles has found her somewhere somewhere. He told her so. That's her brother, Charles, her brother. Goodbye. At last, she feels heavenly hands laying claim to her. Gladly, she gives in. She lets them tow her this way and that, convinced she's being persuaded into the light at last. Goodbye.

Charles has worked hard at making her presentable, but can't get the dishevelment out of her clothes. He would have liked very much to have shown her his personal Naples, but she has never quite come round for him. Undone by those two extra weeks, then worsening. Her slow suffocation, some horror or other making her wring his hand through the night-sweats, saying his name. She never did more than recognise him, repeating the achievement endlessly, happily. And

211

all the while he sits there stupefied, made to look on, too late.

And now that they are free to go, there's no way to make her understand. He's forced to bandy her about, as if her centre had gone soft, her stitching come loose, remonstrating with her when she stumbles against her baggage. He speaks to her like he's holding a sleepy child's shoulders and shaking it, hating himself for saying it. Miss Cotterell nods like a three-quarters drunk, without the peaceful smile. All these locals watching, talking amongst themselves. He feels the humiliation keenly.

Hunched forward in his chair, Keats awaits his turn, patient, fearful. Trite thoughts play on his mind. He watches her go, as though watching his own fate, blinking, expressionless, his hands cradling his kneecaps. There is to be little dignity ahead, then. Charles' servants strain to keep Miss Cotterell high above the crowd, safe, almost raised to shoulder-height, as if revered, an ashen-faced model of Our Lady of Sorrows carried in some local Saints' Day procession, or else, like a fragile, tottering candlestick. Mrs Pidgeon follows after, hurrying along, trying her best to look useful still, her dark skirts dragged across the wet stones.

Naples has thought to send out its neediest souls to greet them. There are plenty of them. They must have little in their lives to be drawn by the spectacle of Miss Cotterell's arrival. They form a ragtag line of washed-up ills, these men, wrapped in damp, woollen blankets, with nothing more than time on their hands down here at the dock. Keats knows the types well from his days in digs in Borough, can put names to most of them: Baleful; Old Whimsy; Hangdog Homespun; Dolour; Skulduggery; and, skulking at the back, Grinning 'Mad' Billy. Their beards are mean and straggly, their hair is smeared to their foreheads, as if it were a stain, a badge of shame they wore: for hire. They all look saddened, slackened, knowing there's nothing much here for them really. A poor show, in all honesty. One or two give him sly looks, but most of them scratch about, hands in pockets, appearing sheepish, feeling their unworthiness, as if they'd been taken and paraded before some great Eastern potentate with a reputation for cruelty and impatience. Not much in the way of rude health here, not much ruddiness. The younger ones, however, are still willing to stare and apprize, carelessly, as if come to weigh the latest imports, see the sick foreigners off their stricken ship, pick the disappointing spoils over. These are the ones, Keats suspects, who, given the opportunity, would come up and nose the taint in him, put fingers in the holes in him. They must wonder what, in England, they feed themselves on, what sort of a climate makes for invalids like these, whole cities peopled with pale ghosts, cringing and frowning and wheezing.

No doubt it's the consequence of spending six weeks out of society, but how Keats dislikes an audience, he realizes more than ever now. It's those eyes of theirs.

213

Once again, it's made clear to him how his clothes have outgrown him. He's sorry for his shabbiness. His greatcoat weighs more heavily now; there's an obvious lack where he used to be. He should have taken more care of himself. Or Severn should. At any rate, someone is at fault; even here, amidst the poorest, the sheen of a man matters, his cut. He's made to feel little better than unladen goods. A soiled, spoiled thing come from afar, made worthless by the getting there. A whimsical curio pointed at in the museum-cabinet. Relics – bones wrapped long ago with great tenderness – that no one believes in any more.

When they see that the Cotterells and Mrs Pidgeon are safely in their carriage, they make their way down. Slowly does it. Keats is watching where he puts his feet. The steps are treacherous here, the pavings broken. He feels his way forward where it's not so slippery. He is supposed to have longed for this, has indeed thoroughly longed for this, his moment of release, his pardon. This is landfall, destination. Yet nothing lets up; all the muscles in his back tense and snarl. Severn tightens his grip. As they suspected, the desperate press in, sensing Keats' uncertainty. Grimed faces leer in at them; hoarse voices make their appeals, their lamentations; a hot hand tugs at Severn's jacket, as though it liked the material. Severn brushes it away, refuses all entreaties. There are soldiers here and there - Swiss guards - but they seem prepared to do nothing, as if they were purely

214

for display, the self-satisfied crowing with power. Keats feels as though they are being handed on through hell, by turns hounded and admired, causing a stir, an enormous heavy sigh trembling after them, pursued by murmurs, envy, jeers. Somebody whistles, as if calling Cerberus. Severn stumbles on, unseeing, hard-hearted, the way mourners do in the cortege, checking his stride only to avoid puddles and slime, picking his way over cobbles and ropes, rusted metal, rubble, till they reach the safety of their hired coach.

Keats is handed in like a shipment of glass, like make-believe. Attempting to get settled in the black, spare interior, he finds himself shaking with relief. Like Severn, he should just close his eyes, recover himself, but no. No stillness in him, he brushes himself down, inspecting the frays on his coat, pulling at a loose thread, whilst trying to believe in his freedom, as if he could banish the horrors of the last ten days in a single tugging gesture. The thread, however, doesn't give up easily.

'Look at this,' he says, the huskiness back in his voice. 'I can't...'

'Can't what?' replies Severn, before he sees what the problem is. Though his own hands are shaking, he quickly succeeds. Keats thanks him.

'And you know what else? It's my birthday today. I thought you'd better know, thought you'd never forgive me if you ever found out.'

215

For several seconds, Severn stares at him, then claps him mightily on the shoulder and laughs, laughs like a man who's got away with it, whatever it may be.

Why say so much? Why roll up the sleeves of his emotions like that and then apply the leeches? He watched Severn fill with amazement and still he couldn't stop. Explanation after explanation. Did he really have to go and tell him everything? Their secret love. Their secret no longer. Like handing a pile of sweat-soaked shirts to a friend, a soiled bag of intimacies. And afterwards, when the sobs had done their work and left him, bowed over, stupid, spent, there was bound to be an awkwardness between them. Severn had the kindness to say little and solve less.

All the same, Keats knows full well that as soon as they agree to pinch out the candle and he lies there, willing sleep in, Severn will be wide awake, staring up at the strange ceiling, eager to set to on what he now knows, nodding to himself, thinking he's understood. There he'll be, tucked up in the darkness, silently playing back their worst conversations, perceived slights and odd scenes, piecing Keats together, making more sense of him than before, reducing him to his lovesickness. And knowing Severn, he'll be up to plenty of good, trying, these next few days, to organise a remedy, a tonic of sorts, some trip out somewhere scenic, – ruins, churches, avenues of trees – expecting to lift his spirits.

And it's not just the inevitable, bitter regret stealing up on him; having told the truth of his feelings, he

217

feels fraudulent, his tongue pushed up against his palate in disgust at himself, since words aren't ever clever or careful enough, no matter how we save them up, polishing and fretting at them. Had he forgotten the value of the unspoken? He might as well have been some penny-dreadful pamphleteer flogging his trumpery at a busy street corner. His word. He can't even remember what he left out. Severn will be having a fine time guessing the rest, smiling, surmising, even now. What made him say it? What made him *begin* to say it and what convinced him he should *keep on* saying it? And saying it in that hoarse, timorous voice, the voice men use to beg for God's mercy. Did he really feel Severn was obscurely owed it, for all his extraordinary, minute attentions? The man had never pried, never second-guessed him. From now on, was there going to be nothing but judgements, allowances, lingering looks of manly fellow-feeling? Outbreaks of pity? Pity? He wishes he could go back to his sickening. Now he will be in the rack for hours.

If he was willing to allow himself a reason, one that could explain such a lapse away, the moment they managed to shut the door to their very own room had a lot to answer for. The fire blazed in the hearth; the bed-linen smelled crisp and fresh; the ceiling, though cracked, dazzled like meringue; there was a well-upholstered chair for each of them and a sturdy table for writing at. Heaven, in short, and a heaven in no danger

218

of pitching or swaying, tilted by the swell. The pleasure of something approaching privacy was as intense as that first bite into the melon they'd had poled aboard – fleshy, orange and warm – when their teethmarks had said it all.

The room had an air of happier times, a peeling gentility; the fabrics had all had their heyday, heavily sat upon by the contented rumps of the lesser English aristocracy. How many had passed through here, toppling into armchairs, easing off tight, muddied boots, exhausted by the puffy-eyed pleasures of too much wealth and high culture, pulling up lazily at the end of their time abroad? Crammed with the names of artefacts and stuffed with things worth knowing, they must have been, their trophies and collections sent on ahead. Time to recover, get a little breath back. The pick of loose-living Naples was spread before them, an inviting, last-course over-indulgence. A fig pudding with cream worth smacking the lips at. Gentlemen could unbutton themselves, reconciled at last to their lusts, knowing that ill-lit streets full of destitute girls were well within reach. Had it been the thought of men like this, ready for England again, that had brought on his weakness?

Either way, he remembers he'd walked in the room like he'd reached his final refuge. He pushed the door to with the finality of a boulder blocking the cave's mouth. The best hotels, by the front, recommended by Charles, had already proved out of the question. These bankers had no idea. Keats and Severn were already down to the affordable, the less desirable. They'd been made to wait for some time in the lobby. Keats had been persuaded to stand there, weak and dispirited, among the spill of trunks and bags, whilst Severn went about the business, bargaining, smoothing several papers on the desk, charming his way to a special price. Keats could feel the sweat cooling on him too quickly, could feel his smile sliding across his face, all athwart. He was aiming at being inconspicuous, casual, just another stupid-sweet, moneyed Englishman at his leisure's end, an incognito. Hopeless. He'd been attracting second looks from every hotelier they'd dealt with.

Was it then the change in circumstances? Or was it more to do with having found himself alone again, away from all the people, the sorry poor all after alms, all wanting a piece of him, a hem of him, the supplicants' awful calling out?

The words, when they came, just forced their way out of him. After all that time he'd kept himself preserved, free from needless confessions, lying stilled and solitary in his bunk, his face to the wooden walls.

No, please, he tells himself, *don't go back there, not back to the ship again.* He promises he'll go to sleep. It will all have been for the best. The room is fine as it is, though there's no view as such, just a sash-window onto the blank grey facade of another hotel, overlooking a narrow alley. It's enough. He's had his fill of horizons, their bluish hazes, the mysterious presentiments of dawn; he's heartily sick of the vast sombre vault of night soaring above him, its cold black cauldron emptying itself of everything.

And Fanny will never know what he's gone and said and Severn, dear Severn, will think no less of him in the morning.

Interview

This is it then; she'll be for it now, called down early to explain herself to the *master*. Not a bad night's sleep, considering, the getting used to it all barely begun, and this impending talk hanging over her. And though she's not been dismissed out of hand, she can fortune-tell well enough when things look bad. And everywhere she looks, they most certainly do. This featureless, half-finished room he's assigned her – no better than servants' quarters – says as much. As did the fretful Miss being taken from her in a great commotion, to be cared for in another wing of the house entirely. 'Out of harm's way,' as the brother put it. But she didn't protest, oh no, but nor did she lower her eyes; he had that look about him – trying for the stern, the forbidding – the whole time in the carriage. In any case, that phrase worked both ways and solitude suited her fine.

Yes, they'd carried Miss in like a rare pearl, like a trophy, as if it were all some great tender homecoming, a cause for celebration, though much good will it do her: the weak thing was too glassy-eyed to take any of it in. His wealth, his good taste, all of it wasted on her. Left alone in the echoey hall, dropped like that, Mrs. Pidgeon couldn't help but notice the doctor about to go after them, no doubt totting up his fee, lining his considerable pockets. No other servants to be seen, all gone off in a palaver. So this was the Palazzo

Cotterell, she'd thought. This villa of his in the classical style revealed almost nothing about him. Or worse, said all there was to know. Cold busts of wise men in white niches. The same tile patterns in an unblinking symmetry. The sturdy, dependable clock ticked on guardedly. No fussy ornament, no extravagance. The whole effect dramatically spartan and comfortless, showily so, as if he were trying too hard to prove a point, show restraint, let the locals know a frugal, scrupulous business would at all times be conducted here. Rigour at the helm of a brisk and burgeoning empire. Whereas she had him down as a penny-pincher.

And now, her future in his lean, white hands, what of that? She knows what to expect. He daren't make much of a scene. References will be given, if ungraciously. And Miss won't be up to saying much, what with all the blacking out. What telling detail will she remember? Best, for all concerned, to keep her strength up, avoid complications. She imagines he will want to be peremptory, exact. The one thing troubling her is, what if he should resent her having been there at the bedside, when he gave way to all those emotions? He wouldn't like too many others to hear of that, she supposes, him being so respected, severe. Even in his fluster, she noticed, even through his sobs, something in him brooked no nonsense.

Once called, she goes straight in. The dimness in there, a mournful, thin light scarcely describing the edges of expensive rectangles – the rug, the paintings, the lofty bookcases – doesn't help her cause. It is a dark, patient den that wants to give little away. All she can deduce is that Mr Cotterell has been smoking. She strains to find him where she'd expect him; he is not in his chair behind the great, glooming desk secured by four thick legs curving down into the floor. Nor is he taking the measure of the garden, by the window. She is beginning to wonder about him – up so early, no paperwork in sight – and is on the point of calling out his name, when, from an unexpected shadow, the whipcrack of his throat-clearing makes her jump. And she'd said she'd be on her guard against him. His voice, lower and deeper, invites her to be seated. There is a straight-backed chair he has put out for her. She folds her hands in her lap and raising her chin, aims a look at him half-defiant, half-demure. Observing her in first light, Charles wonders what his father saw in her, to entrust his daughter's health to this thin-lipped stranger. Then he starts in.

'Mrs Pidgeon, I understand from their letters that my father and my sister had a very high opinion of you, when they first appointed you?'

Mrs Pidgeon shifts slightly in her chair. 'I should say they did, Mr. Cotterell.'

'That they saw a warmth and sympathy in the way you took to my sister more or less immediately?'

Mrs Pidgeon takes her time with this. It's plain

224

he wants her to see where he's headed. She wonders whether she should let him have his say and be done with it: on the whole, yes. 'It's true that I was very struck by her. I recall she seemed so very bright, so – hopeful.'

'Exactly so. All of which leads me to wonder at the recent turn of events, in which, so I have been led to believe, you have proved to be,' – he sees her face thickening, readying itself for a fight – 'forgive me, somewhat less than diligent in your care, to the point, so I understand, at which you could no longer bear to come near my dear sister in her distress?'

'Sir, contrary to what you might or might not have heard, I rarely left your sister's side and when I did, it was as she herself wished, seeing how she so enjoyed the company of the two gentlemen you have met and – I shouldn't wonder – have spoken to about this. At no time was I ever less than attentive. She herself has been so fevered of late, so sluggish and slow to be roused, spent so many hours dead to the world, that for the life of me I can't help but think her memory must have been, in some mysterious ways, playing some of memory's tricks on her.'

'My sister has not said a word to me about any of this. She remains in a very delicate condition. I speak about things that I saw for myself these past few days.'

'Well, sir, I protest I have done my utmost to serve her in what have been most trying circumstances. A month at sea, through storms and calm, with a young

225

woman whose condition was far more serious than I had been led to believe. In a pitiable state she's been, and for some time, as you very well know.'

'What I know, Mrs Pi...'

'If I may continue, sir, I would go so far as to say that unless you yourself had seen what I have seen go on on board that ship and had shared in all our daily, nightly, travails – for they were never less than that – you will be hard pressed to know what I performed out of duty and love.'

Charles has not moved at all through any of this. Now he leans a little forward, rocks a little where he stands, his hands behind his back, impassive, self-contained, yet all the while feeling the cold ooze of outrage spread outward from his brain.

'I have it on good report that there were days, even before you had left England for the last time, when you could barely keep the sneer out of your voice, so denatured had you become, so lacking in any form of compassion for she who depended on your care. From what I hear, you moved about that ship as if Death itself were stalking you, as if one touch, one breath from my poor dear sister would have struck you down. You avoided her, you neglected her, did as little as you could for her, or anyone, and for that alone...'

The chastening goes on. More and more light declares itself. Mr. Cotterell's face grows more and more inflamed, entering the final stages of the tirade. He is

226

moving now all right. Mrs Pidgeon sits there, never saying too much, staring about her as if an enormous space has opened up around her, as if the walls have simply given way and she finds herself outside, before any of this began, among green fields, with the wind on her face, a fierce brightness in her eyes, and every horizon, at tremendous speed, reeling away from her, leaving her emptied and tired and bereft, with nothing worth saying, nothing worth seeing, yet knowing she can at least feel settled now.

Sights

In the end, the day has turned out more solemn than they'd intended. Perhaps each one of them would have preferred other company. Or better still, none. Some relief, at any event, from history, both recent and ancient. And whilst Severn pores over their plans for Rome, trying to make them sound plausible to himself, or else nods in agreement, impressed by every one of Charles' insights, Keats listens to the sounds of another city passing them by. He senses Charles' predicament; the obligations of the host, to spend time with those who, without meaning to, remind him of his sister's helplessness. But they *did* save her life, beyond question. And the good brother turned out to be precisely that, just as Miss Cotterell had foretold. Several times he's told them just how much he's indebted to them. Entirely at their service, he extends his gratitude like a king's white, pampered hand. Which they take, politely, to help pass the time.

And if, at ten o'clock, as promised, there had been an exaggerated grandeur about Charles, a bounce in his step, an over-eagerness to please, his fingers stroking the marbled covers of his guidebook, as if he were about to guarantee marvels, or offer a consultation, then his guests had been quick to understand, make allowances. Miss Cotterell's prospects had further declined. Her brother's hollow cheeks, sucked at like a sour, said as

228

much. Severn commiserated fully. It was a sorrow he knew all about. Besides, the day would be full of other things and Charles would be certain to try not to appear too pensive, calling out orders in expansive Italian, jabbing excitedly at the porticoes they swept past, expounding on the King of Naples' failings, supplying the background to recent, shameful events they might have read about in the newspapers, regarding the constitution. Try and succeed. Keats' and Severn's admiration grew as the day wore on. At every stop, his commentary – a mix of gossip and gardens, politics and the profound – continued apace. The man, it seemed, could go on forever, stricken like this...

'And I think this may interest you, gentlemen, about ten miles from here to the west, in that direction,' Charles flaps a hand vaguely across the rain-dimmed square, 'you'll find Cumae, where, according to legend, the Sybil was imprisoned in a cave.'

'Ah yes, a story we know well, don't we Keats?'

Keats looks where he is told, peering through the drizzle at indistinct hills, misted over, as if absolved. How faraway. 'She could not die,' he replies. 'Yet in the end, she longed for death, hanging in her bottle, shrunken and shrivelled, reduced to nothing more than a voice, the most sought-after voice in the world.'

When he's said this, his friends give him such grave looks, he laughs and runs his hand through his damp hair. 'Hadn't we better go back inside?'

229

Charles is their shepherd. An excellent one. But what Charles has in mind for them, they begin to realize, is an ideal Naples. It can't ever be, Severn wants to tell him. The first squall that comes whipping in from the sea, Charles takes as a personal affront. For fear of disappointing him, Severn assures him the two of them weren't expecting to be as nearly impressed as this. They walk about, gladly at his beck and call, under balconies and archways, through park gates and church doorways, Charles always in front, turning at anything in the least noteworthy or from an earlier century. There's an awful lot of that. Severn and Keats shoot each other smiles. For a time, Keats is well enough to stroll on a little, lengthening his stride, shaking the words off like droplets from unseasonal showers. The sun even comes out for a while.

Fortunately, by late afternoon, once the rain has properly set in, the carriage rattles on through the suburbs without stopping, and there are times, blessedly drawn out, when, as if by silent consent, nothing need be remarked on or alluded to again. Keats keeps his forehead against the window. If he should sigh, then no one will hear him. At a shudder of his, the other two will shift about for his comfort, contrive more room for his little leaden shape. He can even close his eyes, and forget about the sights...

Later on, at Charles' absolute insistence, they draw up outside the Chiesa Nuova di Gesu. They must see

one church before they go home. From the outside, forthright and forbidding, it looks like a bank. Inside, in a dim chapel's failing light, Keats finds himself alone, at last, and lets himself down gently to his knees behind some dark pew. Overcome by overwrought scrollwork, a statue of Our Lady weeps and languishes there. Plaster and gilt. He won't pray; he just keeps repeating, 'Not long now', almost contentedly. For isn't there comfort in that? After a while, he hears the stiffness in Severn's old boots clump down the aisle: probably looking for him already. He'd better get up. Around him, veils of soft gloom linger in the quiet. He ghost-glides through vapours as chilling as a sea-fog. *Never himself fully again* – he hasn't forgotten. All these saints are no better than strangers to him. He sees them up there in their niches, the martyrs, long-suffering, disconcertingly attached to their methods of torture; their seeled eyes rightly pour their scorn down on him. As he gets to his feet, he senses they will always be superior – next to theirs, his own coming trials seem trivial. And now he's back in his head where he's not supposed to be, giving himself a matter of weeks.

Across from him, he can see Severn and Charles in some earnest discussion, the pair of them stooped with shared compassion, and he suddenly feels sorry for them. Mrs Pidgeon has had to be dismissed; Charles has booked her return passage. As for Miss Cotterell, she sits for long periods gazing at the garden, numb and silent and wan,

231

unable to identify a single plant or shrub. When Charles comes to speak with her, he finds her asleep in her chair, dreaming. The doctors come every day. She smiles weakly and submits. And so it resumes. Severn's hand is clapped on Charles' shoulder, his other hand chopping at the air, deftly encouraging – or berating – him. They are deep in either his or Miss Cotterell's downfall, Keats supposes, turning one of them over like a pitchfork into hay. He no longer minds. No need to hear what they have to say. He knows it already. *Never himself fully again*.

'She says it's not what she expected,' Charles is saying. 'She says it will never do for home. She doesn't want to know the servants' names, what the dishes they bring her are called, the names of the flowers I've had arranged on the table.'

'Perhaps she needs more time?'

'But that's precisely what I'm afraid of.'

'And the doctor? What does he intend to do about this? Is it in anyway unusual? I could always ask Keats.'

'Best not. The two of you have helped all you can. Besides, it's not more opinions that she needs. I was hoping that a few days' rest in a proper house would have made a difference. Or that her brother's company would revive her.'

Charles makes a face.

'No, you mustn't take it like that. She talked of nothing but you each and every day; you were first in her prayers.'

'I've not heard her pray since I brought her ashore.'

232

'But that doesn't mean...'

'If you saw the way she looks, or rather doesn't look, doesn't look up or take anything in.'

They break off; Keats is coming over.

On the road

It's worse than execrable and exactly what everyone warned them, though the telling is never warning enough. Travel as travail; going as undergoing, steep after steep. Yet wasn't it always like this? And would be till the end? Out here in the wilderness, it's not the bandits that lie in wait but the road itself.

It was funny at first, capering about like vaudevillians in a confusion of coats and cushions as the vettura – a considerable expense, meant to be one last luxury – jolted and shuddered along, but about ten miles out of Naples, climbing steadily, the surface disintegrated, and the road simply gave out, gave up all claims to be road. Nothing resembled itself any more.

In no time at all, they felt bullied, repeatedly clattered about the head by a bare-knuckled big-hitter. Keats for one soon tired of scrambling up the scree of himself, holding his insides together, picking his way out of the debris, the rockfall. They felt like two hazelnuts in a walnut's shell, a pair of blackened pennies in a beggar's cup: how many times had they been flung into each other's arms, or dumped sprawling on the floor, groping about for their dignity? It was fortunate they had nothing left to keep from each other.

Between ricochets, to stop himself tensing and hunching, Keats went on tunelessly composing comic doggerel. Otherwise, he worried about the burden

he'd become. A stark death's-head wrapped up for the final off. His teeth coming loose. The beginnings of mummification. Reduced to skin and bone and will, an animal cussedness. Severn had promised he would not pity him, not even at the last, and was keeping to it. Poor man, he hadn't sketched a thing since they set out for Rome; overnighting at disappointing inns, he complained of headaches, bad eyesight, seeing things. The country roundabout didn't agree with him. Too much dust and poverty; one clay-coloured village after another tumbling down the hillside. Disgruntlements everywhere they stopped. Stupid arguments over money, the state of the bed-linen. Nor could Severn rid himself of his fear of bandits; though Keats joked about it, it was true: the two of them could have raised a pretty sum, even in their unhappy condition. Of all this Severn tried to show as little as possible, having learnt restraint from his friend.

Now, just this one last slow climb and, perhaps, these troublesome hills will be behind them for good. Over too, their grinding slog through them, at little more than walking pace, the horses dragging their hooves, as obstinate as Keats himself. Their progress painfully uneven, uneventful. Not one sign of a precipice along the way, no dizzying void to concern them. They're not that sort of hills. Rather, relentless plod, the driver nudging them forwards, taking his time. More views, like the ones they've forgotten already, slip by.

Keats sits like an ashen, miserable pasha, wisely saying nothing, surrounded by cushions, tended by his friend. The back of Severn's head, half-coddled in a blanket which keeps slipping down, is repeatedly banged against the side of the vettura; he feels every pothole like a personal affront. Injuries all over. Part of him longs for the spectacular axle-breaking rut that would send them sprawling, put an end to these tortures of theirs.

'You're not saying much today,' Keats says. Normally when Severn climbs back in, having stretched his legs and taken the air, having given Keats much-needed napping-room, he has seen something else to draw his friend's attention to: a spray of wild flowers; the gnarled trunks of an olive grove; promising cloud patterns; new dialect words he's asked the driver to explain; a difficult gradient ahead; anything. He's become Keats' interpreter of the world, fetching surprises for him. Today he has come back empty-handed.

'Must be the company I keep.'

'And there I was just thinking how well I'd been feeling.'

'You do seem more yourself today, it's true.'

They fall silent for a while. Severn taps his fingers against his lips, forming a question:

'Do you ever get the feeling we might've taken the wrong turn?'

'All the time,' grins Keats. 'What makes you say that?'

236

'I've been thinking about my father a lot lately. Whether he'll ever be the same should I return...'

'My God, Severn, you really are in capital spirits this morning.'

'Yes, well, be careful then. They may be catching.'

'Don't be like that. May I remind you it's my spirits you're supposed to be keeping up?'

'If it makes you feel any better, I admit I've been thinking a great deal about this landscape, too, this extraordinary autumn we're going through. How, in terms of colours, does it compare to Scotland, would you say?'

'I'd say the locals are far more intelligible.'

With that, Keats closes his eyes. Severn smiles to himself. Even now, Keats still manages to have the last word. He looks over at his ailing friend. Let him be now.

Suddenly, the vettura pulls up in a violent protestation of the most comprehensive heaving and wheezing, then moodily hunkers down, as if settling back into its dusty black shell and refusing to come out. They must have reached the summit. The wheels to and fro in a shallow, dry rut. Hiatus. They hear the driver jump down, muttering to himself.

'Whatever now?' asks Keats in exasperation, more pain coming on.

Without a word, their driver goes off to stretch out under some trees, lights his pipe carefully. Behind him, the subdued, sticky breathing of done-for horses.

237

Crickets exploit the last of the warmth. Desultory puffs of clouds, making for home. Evening is miles away. In the vettura, an argument breaks out – 'I said I've had enough!' – followed by the prolonged silence of men not wanting to admit they're wrong. Neither Severn nor Keats seems in a hurry to get out; they stare out of opposite windows. At last the door swings open, like the slow passing of a judgement.

Severn steps out, full of consternation, dabbing at his temples.

'You shouldn't be saying things like that,' Keats calls out after him. 'There's no excuse. No need.'

That brave face Severn's put on so often needs repairing. He feels its stiffening clays starting to crack; the confidant's rictus. What's left to say to Keats when he works himself up like this? They simply have to go on; surely Keats must know that. He swishes his way through the bracken, off for a long, angry piss.

Keats, meanwhile, having pulled himself together, hesitates briefly at the big step down to the dusty ground, wondering if can he make it on his own. He steadies himself, resolves to make instant amends. He heads for the driver to find out how far they have left to go today, sits down gingerly in a tall tree's shadow. Eventually, Severn comes back, says nothing, hands in pockets, waiting. Keats senses he's been forgiven, waves to him to join them.

It ought to be a common traveller's scene, familiar

238

the world over, men lounging at the roadside, pointing out the way they've come, wondering about the hospitality at the inn ahead. Keats looks out at the panorama, wants to see as much as he can. Before him, the campagna stretches, dispiritingly empty and flat.

He straightens with an effort, turns to face Severn. Dear Severn. He starts to say something, then thinks better of it. Surely by now, his look should say everything, but he knows his eyes have no light left in them.

'I'm sorry,' he says. 'Let's do as you say and get back in.'

EPILOGUE: 1821

Graveside

There's a plot of land no one wants, almost wild, that they've been allowed to use, consecrated ground. The husband and wife who live nearby say they'll tend it for very little money, but he's not convinced. Few people come out this far to check.

Nevertheless, despite everything, here are the flowers of early spring, in abundance, swathes of their frail striving. He had not expected to see them, certainly not so many. They seem quite happy with themselves, well-established, compliant. Their cups open to the sun. For all he knows, they could be saying little fragrant prayers all day long.

Charles has brought nothing with him today. Nothing but his heaviness, a new blindness in him. He pauses on the muddy path and looks about him, reading 'Here lies Margaret Wildsmith, the best of mothers, taken from us on the 12th of July, 1818.' Ragged primroses over her. What children forget...

He sets off again, headed for the hedgerow at the far end of the plot. North-facing. Spring hasn't reached her yet, though she's waiting. She was always prepared to be patient, wasn't she? He can't answer. He knows he barely knew her. After last night's rain, the ground is somewhat soft; his black boots leave wet prints in the grass as he strides out to meet her. Here she is, just as he left her. Here are the flowers from yesterday, the flowers of early spring. He stoops to brush some raindrops off the stone then stands back and rereads what he chose to have engraved. They are simple enough. 'Clare Cotterell, beloved sister, sorely missed. 1804 -1821.'

From Dr Clark's notes, Rome.

What a scene of devastation!
Worse than I'd previously encountered.
Both lungs completely gone, saturated, as if drowned.
Dreadful to behold.
Considerable pulmonary damage everywhere.
Black mass of putrefaction.
No need to further examine either stomach or intestinal
canal.

Afterword

In this book, I have tried to stick to the known facts about Keats' journey from England to Italy. All the key information – names, dates and places – comes from contemporary letters and recollections and from the major biographies of Keats. The rest I made up.

Richard Boden, October 2019

www.ingramcontent.com/pod-product-compliance
Lightning Source LLC
Chambersburg PA
CBHW060422180626
46817CB00007B/2623